CUBA
15

CUBA 15

a novel by
Nancy Osa

delacorte press

Published by
Delacorte Press
an imprint of
Random House Children's Books
a division of Random House, Inc.
New York

Visit us on the Web! www.randomhouse.com/teens
Educators and librarians, for a variety of teaching tools, visit us at
www.randomhouse.com/teachers

Library of Congress Cataloging-in-Publication Data
Osa, Nancy.
Cuba 15 / Nancy Osa.
p.   cm.
Summary: Violet Paz, a Chicago high school student,
reluctantly prepares for her upcoming "quince," a Spanish nickname
for the celebration of a Hispanic girl's fifteenth birthday.
ISBN 0-385-73021-7–ISBN 0-385-90086-4 (lib. bdg.)
1. Cuban Americans–Juvenile fiction. [1. Cuban Americans–Fiction.
2. Quinceañero (Social custom)–Fiction. 3. High schools–Fiction.
4. Schools–Fiction.] I. Title. II. Title: Cuba fifteen.
PZ7.O785Cu 2003
[Fic]–dc21
2002013389

The text of this book is set in 11.5-point Baskerville BE.

Book design by Angela Carlino

Printed in the United States of America

June 2003

10 9 8 7 6 5 4

BVG

Para mi familia,
aquí y allá

Acknowledgments

Millón de gracias to the Hedgebrook Foundation and my Hedgemates; my talented editor, Françoise Bui; my book-loving family; Keith Gaylor; ACME Writers; Professor Craig Clinton; and speech and Spanish teachers everywhere.

Author's Note

The *quinceañero (KEEN-say-ahn-YEH-ro)*, or *quince*, is a fifteenth-year coming-of-age ceremony traditionally held for girls in Latin American countries. The girl being honored is sometimes called the *quinceañera*. Customs and spellings vary among different ethnic groups, but the purpose of guiding young women to adulthood remains the same.

–N.O.

1

What can be funny about having to stand up in front of everyone you know, in a ruffly dress the color of Pepto-Bismol, and proclaim your womanhood? Nothing. *Nada.* Zip. Not when you're fifteen–too young to drive, win the lottery, or vote for a president who might lower the driving and gambling ages. Nothing funny at all. At least that's what I thought in September.

My–*womanhoods*–hadn't even begun to grow; I wore a bra size so small they'd named it with lowercase letters: *aaa.* Guys avoided me like the feminine hygiene aisle at the grocery store. And I never wore dresses. Not since I'd left school uniforms behind. Not ever, no exceptions. You'd think my own grandmother would remember that.

She didn't.

"*Eh,* Violet, *m'ija.* I want buy you a gown and make you a 'keen-say' party," my grandmother said early that September morning in her customized English, shrewdly springing her idea on me at breakfast.

"Sounds good, Abuela," I said as I buttered my muffin. "Except for the dress."

Just Abuela, my little brother, Mark, and I were up; Abuelo, tired from traveling, was sleeping in, and Mom never got up until after Mark and I had left for school. Thrift store worker's hours. Mom ran the Rise & Walk Thrift Sanctuary, a used-clothing shop in the church basement that operates on donations. Their motto is "The Threads Shall Walk Again." Dad was on the early shift at the twenty-four-hour pharmacy inside the Lincolnville Food Depot, a combination grocery store/bank/hairdresser/veterinary hospital/pharmacy/service station. All they needed now was a tattoo parlor.

"What's 'keent-sy'?" Mark asked, adding, "I want one too!"

"The *quince,*" said Abuela, "this is short for *quinceañero,* the fifteenth birthday in Cuba." She pronounced it "Coo-ba," the Spanish way. "Is a ceremony only for the girls," she added, shaking a finger at Mark, who tipped his cereal bowl toward his mouth to get the last of the sugary milk at the bottom.

He swallowed. "That's sexist, Abuela. Only for girls." He tried another pass at his cereal bowl, but it was empty. "I know, because last year in my school on Take Your

2

Daughters to Work Day, Father Leone said sons got to go to work too. So I got out of school!"

Abuela, looking starched somehow in one of Mom's old terry cloth robes, her silver hair in a bun, raised an eyebrow and gave a wry smile. "This is equality, yes?"

She often says yes when she means no, and vice versa.

"The *quinceañero, m'ijo,* this is the time when the girl becomes the woman."

Mark, who was eleven then, shied away from any discussion that even hinted at having to do with body parts or workings. He turned corpuscle red, a nice counterpoint to his royal blue Cubs baseball cap, which he wore all day every day during the pro season, except in school and church, until the end of the last game of the World Series. The fringe of his dark hair stuck out in a ragged halo around his face. He immediately lost interest in the *quince* party. "Nevermind, countmeout," he mumbled.

Abuela didn't notice. "The *quince* is the time when all the *resto del mundo* ass-cepts your dear sister as an adult in the eyes of God and family. And she, in turn, promises to ass-cept *responsabilidad* for all the wonders in the world of adults."

Responsabilidad. This sank in as deeply as the Country Crock into the nooks and crannies of my half-eaten English muffin, and raised a red flag. This *quince* party could be some sort of trap. "What if I don't want to—ass-cept more responsibilities?" I asked, mindlessly mimicking Abuela's pronunciation.

Mark slipped away, leaving his empty cereal bowl and milk glass on the table.

Abuela sat down with a tiny cup of sweet, black coffee.

"*Responsabilidades*—how do you say? These come with the territory, *chiquitica*." She downed her coffee in one shot.

I pointed to Mark's dirty bowl. "How about *his* responsibilities?"

She shrugged and motioned for me to clear his place.

"Now *that's* sexist," I grumbled, stomping off to the sink with Mark's dishes and my own.

Abuela said something that rhymed in Spanish, then translated: "The bull cannot make the milk, and the cow alone cannot make the bull."

I kissed her, shaking my head, and left for school. There's no sense arguing with the fundamentals.

★　★　★

Leda Lundquist stood waiting for me outside Spanish class. My friend Leda is as slim as a sunflower and admirably as tall, though not quite as seedy. She has long, straight, pale-pale blond hair and white-white skin with just the faintest glow to indicate that blood does run through her veins.

"Yo, Paz," she said to me at the door, with her usual lack of finesse. "Come away with me this weekend."

"Don't you have a boyfriend for that, Leed?" I asked, sweeping past her and into the last row of seats.

Leda set down her gym duffel and books and sat beside me, braiding her hair into an orderly rope. She wore a giant turquoise tie-dyed T-shirt as a dress, belted with a rolled-up bandana. Rubber flip-flops and a pink plastic Slinky on one arm for a bracelet completed her back-to-school look. "I have got the perfect fund-raiser for you—for us—to go to Saturday afternoon."

I groaned. "No way," I said, before she had a chance to state her case.

"C-U-B-A" was all she said, and she waited for my reaction.

I raised my eyebrows in a let-me-have-it look.

"The Cuba Caravan's coming through town. Isn't your dad going? There's gonna be a dance, and a send-off, and–"

I shook my head no, and harder for no way. I didn't want to stir up that kettle of Caribbean fish. The subject of Cuba was best left unmentioned around Dad. "Forget it, Leda," I said, wondering how many times I'd been caught up in this constant refusal of invitations since we'd first met. With the Lundquists' raft of causes, most weekends offered at least one political demonstration for the family to enjoy.

"–and even a *raffle*, Paz, what could be better than that? Besides . . ."

She paused.

"Besides what?"

"Well . . . if we stand around long enough, you might meet some hunky Cuban guys at the salsa dance . . . and I could top a thousand bucks in the walkabout fund."

Aha. The true motive. Leda was speaking of the European adventure fund that her parents pay into every time she goes to some activist thing with them–double if she brings a friend. By the time she turns eighteen, Leda plans to have enough money to traipse across Europe and several other continents, solo.

Which was why we, lofty sophomore creatures that we were, presently found ourselves in the back row of Señora

5

Wong's freshman Spanish class, trying not to be noticed. It had been Leda's idea to take the first year of each language offered at Tri-District High so she'd be able to speak a little of the native tongue no matter where she roamed. Last year, *merci beaucoup,* it had been French. I didn't care which language I learned, so I tagged along for the fun of it.

Señora Wong, diminutive but not fragile, ruled with an ironic fist. "Leona, Violeta, could you find it in your hearts to join the rest of us?" she asked, calling us by our Spanish-class names, hitting just the right note of sarcasm. She went on to show the class the same list of easy nouns that Leda and I learned last year at this time: *casa, sombrero, estudiante*—only last year it was in French.

I tuned her out and thought again about Leda's proposal for the weekend. If I did go, the *déjà vu* factor would be high. A grin escaped me as I remembered our first meeting, at a peace rally in Grant Park, back when I was still in eighth grade. I had tagged along with my aunt Luz— Dad's little sister—who was in town, taking pictures on assignment. Tía Luci had handed me a PEACE NOW! poster to wave and moved off to snap some photos. Caught up in the pulsating crowd, I was feeling a little overwhelmed when a concerned voice at my elbow asked, "Are you okay?"

The voice belonged to a tall girl with long white-blond hair and the skinniest arms and legs I had ever seen. Was *I* okay?

"Of course I am," I blustered, too embarrassed to admit I was afraid of being on my own among the marchers. "Great rally, huh?" I said, shoving my poster back out in front of me.

"I've seen better," came the blasé reply. As the girl leaned over to slurp from a push-button water fountain, her long straight hair fell from a bandana tied pirate-style over the top of her head. A peasant shirt with the sleeves cut out flapped over skintight leggings, which had been cut roughly at the knee. All of this perched precariously atop two stork-on-a-diet legs. She straightened up, wiping her lips with a fist. "Redwood Summer was pretty wild," she said. "I'm Leda. And you are . . . ?"

"Violet."

"Violet, huh? Violet!" She gazed deeply into my eyes through ice-blue ones. "I have something very important to tell you."

Who *was* this person? Why was she staring at me?

"MON ECAEP?" She pointed gravely to my middle. "Your sign's upside down."

So it was. How long had I been holding PEACE NOW! upside down? Embarrassed twice in two minutes—and by a twelve-year-old! I asked Leda which grade she was in first, but she said her school didn't have grades. She would be thirteen at the end of August.

"Let's make a point of keeping in touch," she'd said at the end of the day, as though she networked like this all the time. *Let's keep in touch.* No one had ever said that to me before. So we got to be friends.

Leda was unlike any of my Catholic-school classmates. She called her parents by their first names and went to an alternative school. She demonstrated on the weekends at political rallies. And she was a vegetarian. I had never met a vegetarian before. Even Jesus ate meat, we were taught. Or at least fish.

Our differences only drew Leda and me to each other until we sort of fed off them, like those relationships where one fish scrapes dead barnacles off the other. But we were alike in some ways. Neither of us could dance. We liked to ski, and we hated video games and football. Plus, we'd both had to go along with a lifetime of our families' crazy schemes, something we couldn't wait to escape.

Now, two years after meeting, with both of us in public high school and Leda's around-the-world tour looming, my friend had found her own capitalist cause within her parents' causes. I decided to go with her on Saturday; I could tell Dad the Cuba fund-raiser was for some other benefit. Since I didn't have any plans for the future, I figured helping to send Leda around the world was the least I could do. And if I met some hunky Cuban guy at the same time, well, I'd call it a birthday present.

"Muy bien," I surrendered to Leda after class. "You win."

"What?"

"I'll go with you to the Cuba thing."

She blinked at me. "Was it the hunk part that convinced you?"

"Is that all you think about?"

Leda tossed her braid over her shoulder. "Try to."

2

That afternoon, Abuela lay in wait.

"I don't like to wear dresses anymore," I said, sitting down at the piano in the living room to practice. I trilled over a few keys. "Don't you remember?"

"No, *mi palomita*," Abuela said, shaking her coiffed, silver-haired head. A Spanish-language magazine sat open on her perfectly ironed lap—her paisley skirt, in swirling shades of green, stayed crisp even though it was made of a shimmery, silky fabric. Abuela always looks as though she's just peeled off the dry cleaner's protective plastic bag. Her raucous makeup is the only chink in her otherwise solid look of togetherness.

"Ven acá, chica," she said, beckoning.

When I joined her on the couch, she tapped the centerfold spread in front of us: a backlit photo of a disembodied floor-length evening gown, the kind Cinderella's stepsisters might have worn if they'd had less taste. "This dress, it is the *estilo tradicional,"* Abuela said, as though that made it okay.

The dress went from long sleeves to a high neckline in a horrible clash of textures. From its starched, pink taffeta thorax dripped lacy pink ruffles, pink buttons, pink beads. It dripped—*pink.*

"Tradicional," Abuela repeated, tapping the page.

Pink was traditional? I couldn't plead ignorance-as-usual and say *No comprendo,* because this time I understood her Spanish, but only because she'd used a cognate. And I only knew what cognates were because Señora Wong had defined them on the first day of class, to demonstrate to us clueless *estudiantes* how much of the language we already knew: *mucho.* So instead I said to my grandmother, "This dress . . . it's . . . nice," and cocked my head at an angle, trying to find some truth to my words.

"Bueno," replied Abuela. A bright smile bloomed on her shockingly orange-painted lips. "We plan the *fiestecita* for next *eh*spring. My little Violeta is becoming *una mujer!"* She sounded so satisfied that I couldn't say no just then. Besides, I'd used up all my arguments already.

I had pointed out that it wouldn't be a real birthday party because I was *already* fifteen years old—that's why she was here in the first place. We had celebrated my birthday the night before. Abuela and Abuelo, Dad's parents, visit us twice every year, in September for my birthday and in May for Dad's. They say those are the only months of the year when the Chicago area is habitable—on account of the snow, the wind off the lake, and, they emphasize, rolling their *rs*, "that *ter-r-r-ri-ble humedad.*" Yes, the humidity. And they live in Miami.

But Abuela informed me that the *quince* party need only take place sometime during the year in which one turns fifteen. The girl gets a new dress and a tiara, a bunch of pictures taken in them, and a huge party at a rented hall with all her friends and relatives invited. *A tiara.* These rules had been drawn up in Cuba, and I figured they were pretty strictly enforced, because Abuela seemed to know exactly what she was talking about, and there didn't appear to be much leeway. I was going to have a party in May whether I liked it or not. Judging from the magazine photos, I'd be wearing this pink monster of a dress and a Miss America crown, clutching the arm of some pimply cousin I barely knew, and tottering onto a stage in front of God and everyone else, proclaiming *I am Woman.*

The horror.

How could I tell my own grandmother that I hated dresses, wouldn't be caught dead onstage, and didn't even think of myself as Cuban? I had green eyes and practically blond hair, for God's sake—the same coloring as my Polish American mother.

"Okay, Abuela," I murmured instead.

From the hallway came the singular *veep-veep!* of acetate on acetate. My mom, Diane Shavlovsky Paz, zipped into view.

"Did I hear someone mention a party?" Mom wore a teal, white, and fuchsia "running" suit top decorated with asymmetrical, eye-bruising graphics, and a pair of pale yellow sweatpants outlined with silver piping. Huge clip-on gold hoops hung from her ears; they swung in aftershock for a full thirty seconds after she sat down across from us, in the white wicker armchair with the red velvet upholstery. She propped her gold open-toed sandals up on the kidney-shaped glass coffee table.

Our house is decorated in Spanish Colonial meets Early Thrift Shop, and so, it seemed, was my mother today. She doesn't always look this good. "Fashion is not my long suit," she'll often say, followed by a pregnant pause while she waits for me to get the pun.

"Your hair looks nice, Mom," I said, trying to divert her attention.

"Thanks, Vi. Now, have you set a date yet?"

"A date?" Great. This was beginning to sound like a wedding. And, as I mentioned, my love life lay at an all-time low. They'd have to get me one of those mail-order husbands. Or, if he were coming from Cuba, I guessed you'd call him a *sail*-order husband. Because of the raft deal.

Abuela doesn't like talking about the rafters. So I didn't tell my joke, though Mom would have loved it.

"*Sí,*" said Abuela, nodding, "we must make the date for the rental of the hall." She murmured something in Spanish to Mom, who is fluent; I only caught *ella* and *especial.* Then I felt a small yet strong lightning-flash shoot between them, and through the charged air whistling past, I heard Mom say the word. In English. And I knew I was finished.

"Planning!" said Mom. "It's all in the planning. We pick the date and work backwards from there." She should know; Mom has planned umpteen grand openings for a restaurant that has yet to make it off the drawing board.

"Wh-what's to plan?" I asked nervously. "Invite a couple friends, set up a few folding chairs, and bam!"

"I give you 'bam'!" retorted Abuela. "The *quinceañero* requires *muchos planes*–for the invitations, for the fittings, for to choose the band . . ."

"And planning," my mother, in her mismatched ensemble, reminded us, "is my long suit."

There was no arguing that point. Planning was my mother's great hobby. The thing she had trouble with, according to the vocabulary word I looked up because I missed it on the English pretest, was *fruition*. So maybe this shindig would never really happen. It was practically my only hope.

Abuela had opened her electronic notebook. "The last weekend in May," she said, scrolling through her computerized calendar, "would be *perfecto*."

Mom reached under a cushion and pulled out our family calendar, the new one from St. Edna's Church that showed a picture of a different local celebrity receiving Communion for each month of the year. From behind her ear, she produced a thick black marker that advertised BUSTER'S MEATS.

Where had those come from? If I didn't know better, I'd have thought Mom and Abuela had been plotting this ambush for quite some time. Abuela is especially canny that way. But Mom wouldn't do that to me. She knows I feel like a dork in dresses. When I vowed on eighth-grade graduation day never again to be hemmed in by a skirt, Mom agreed. "Everyone's got to develop their own style," she said. So I was sure she'd understand.

She raised an eyebrow at Abuela. "Saturday?"

"Domingo es tradicional."

"Sunday it is!" Mom flipped through the calendar months to May. Beneath the profile of a well-known professional football coach sticking his pink and gray tongue out to receive the Host, in the next-to-last square on the page, she wrote in indelible black ink: VIOLET'S QUINCE PARTY.

So much for Mom's unwavering support.

A nervous chuckle rose up in me, but I refused to let it out. It rattled around inside for a minute, then died. This *quince* business was no laughing matter.

3

The next afternoon, I gave my first presentation in Ms. Joyner's speech class. It was the strangest thing: I couldn't stand meeting anyone as myself, but I never minded performing as another character. As long as I wasn't all alone onstage. Violet Paz, the great impostor. I just fuzzed everyone out by unfocusing my eyes, and, bingo! I was fine. Unfortunately, this doesn't work when shaking hands with a stranger. It doesn't work in speech performance either, as I would soon find out.

Ms. Joyner had assigned a scene from *The Importance of Being Earnest* to me and my old friend Janell Kelly. We'd known each other since the first grade at St. Edna's

Elementary. The two of us had put together many a skit in eight years in the same classroom. Our most memorable collaboration was for a religion assignment in second grade, a song we wrote to the tune of "Hello, Dolly!" entitled "Hello, Yahweh!" It was lucky we had the lay teacher that year.

This year, speech was the only class period Janell and I shared. Besides geometry and English, Janell was studying music (French horn), dance, and martial arts first semester— maybe prepping for a career in performance art. But she was performing rather badly now.

" 'Cecily,' " Janell's Gwendolen Fairfax warbled in a bad British accent, " 'mamma, whose views on education are remarkably strict, has brought me up to be extremely short-sighted; it is part of her system; so do you mind my looking at you through my glasses?' " She forgot to pantomime, playing Gwendolen's sarcasm with the humorlessness of Queen Elizabeth with a bad tooth, and the pun was lost. Janell took deadpan far too seriously.

While the class applauded with scorn, our teacher sat on the floor, writing on her clipboard. Willow thin, with medium-chocolate coloring and permed hair that hugs her head, Ms. Joyner is the bright bird in the drab nest that is Tri-Dist. The classroom walls in C wing are all painted a yellow so wan it puts you to sleep. Unless you're in Ms. Joyner's class. Today, she wore a billowy kind of jumpsuit with different-colored jewels and gems silk-screened all over it. Ms. Joyner is the only teacher I know who dresses better than her students, and that's saying a lot.

Janell's and my presentation had been last, so people

started filing out with the bell. We waited for the okay from Ms. Joyner, who had told everyone "Nice job" after their performance. But she still sat cross-legged up against a side wall, scribbling on her clipboard.

We had just given each other the let's-go shrug when Ms. Joyner spoke. "Not so fast, girls," she said in her rich tenor, still writing. She underlined something real heavy, folded the bright pink sheet, and handed it to me with a smile. "I'd like you two to go see Mr. Axelrod in his office. He knows you're coming."

Mr. Axelrod? The head of the speech department? Better known as The Ax? Janell and I stared at each other wide-eyed.

"Now," commanded Ms. Joyner, smile fading. She got up in one billowing motion and escorted us to the door.

★   ★   ★

"Was the scene that rotten?" I whispered to Janell on our way down the hall.

"I didn't know you could get punished for bad acting," she said. "Man, speech teachers are strict." She lashed out with a tae-kwon-do kick, and I automatically fell back a length.

As I dawdled and Janell whirled, a door opened and a cold shadow fell across the hall, stopping us dead in our tracks. A tall, well-built man with a craggy face and longish black hair pulled back in a ponytail blocked our path. He had on khaki Dockers and an old dark cable-knit sweater with pills on it, and those brown rubber-soled shoes that guy teachers wear. The tiniest sliver of a gold earring hung from one ear like a very expensive sickle.

He stood, looking us over, one dark eyebrow cocked,

for what seemed like the rest of my life. The second hand on the hall clock shivered and froze. The slams of lockers and the chirps of birds outside died. Wordlessly, the man pointed a finger at Janell and me, then back at his office.

The Ax. And he wanted us.

Dutifully we marched in, and I handed him Ms. Joyner's note. He glanced at it, motioned for us to remain standing.

"Mr. Axelrod, I can explain—" Janell began. He stopped her with a half-raised palm and seated himself behind his desk. A large trophy and several smaller ones glistened in a glass case on the wall.

"You," he said to me.

I stood stock-still as he absorbed my features—my five-feet-two, hundred-pound-weakling frame, the shoulder-length dirty-blond hair I inherited from Mom that won't hold a curl, the emerald green eyes that are my one and only best asset.

"Walk," he said, waving me across the tiny room. "You too," he said to Janell.

It was easily the clumsiest walk I'd taken in weeks, months, years—since I'd tripped over my graduation robe and smacked into Father Leone while receiving my eighth-grade diploma. I tried to force my tennis shoes into a straight line as Janell shifted into her dancer's glide, passing me on her way back to where we'd started. Incredible. We were dressed alike in T-shirts and jeans, but Janell had suddenly become Ginger Rogers versus my Lucille Ball.

"You," said Mr. Axelrod to me again, boring into my eyes this time, "are funny."

I wasn't *that* funny.

"You," he grunted at Janell, "are not."

This was not news.

A light like a camera-flash passed over his face—a vague try at a smile—and was gone. "Ms. Joyner recommended you girls. We need a few live bodies to round out our speech team this year." It wasn't a question.

"You," he pointed at me. "Original Comedy. Write your name on the sign-up sheet outside."

I dared to open my mouth. "Original what?"

The Ax lobotomized me with a look. "Comedy," he said, not laughing. "Your event. And you." He locked eyes with Janell. "Dramatic Interp. No! Wait!"

We did.

"What do you know about poetry?" he asked her.

"Nothing," she replied.

"That's your event. Verse Reading," he said, ending the interview. "Sign up outside. Team meeting's Saturday at two. Be there."

★　★　★

Saturday was the day of Leda's fund-raiser. I'd have to cancel. I tried calling her as soon as I got home from school, but her line was busy. The Lundquists don't believe in call-waiting.

When I finally got through, Leda said, "I was just trying to call you, dude! Too cosmic. Look, Paz, I've got to cancel out on Saturday. I mean, you can still go by yourself if you want—"

"Wait a minute," I said. "I can't go either. Me and Janell got in some kind of trouble during speech today, and we have to show up at this meeting—"

"Saturday at two o'clock!" she finished for me. "You're joining the team too?"

"What?"

"Speech team, Paz. Do I have to spell it out for you?"

"But your parents never let you join after-school clubs. On account of the weekend warrior thing. What the heck's going on?"

"Got lucky, I guess. I gave that animal-rights speech in class this morning?" Leda took Intro Speech another period. "Well, Ms. Joyner says I'm a natural for Original Oratory."

"So, did you have to talk to The Ax?"

"Yeah, met him. He's extremely cool. That earring?"

I shivered, remembering it. "It looked *sharp,* for one thing. He could probably cut your heart out with it," I said. "Why do you think they call him The Ax? And why are Beth and Niles letting you do this?"

Leda's voice clouded with paranoia; one of her parents must have been hovering nearby. "Paz," she said low, "this is the greatest: If I write orations on the Causes, the units say they'll pay me for every speech tournament." Speech team. Leda's parental units had found another outlet for their message.

Leda sighed. "If I never have to go to another telephone-tree potluck, it'll be too soon."

"Well," I said ruefully, "I probably wouldn't have met any hunky Cuban guys this weekend anyway. I hate meeting strangers."

"Then how're you ever going to meet any new guys?" Leda made my allergy to strangers sound like a mortal sin.

"Maybe there'll be some cute ones on the speech team," I said halfheartedly. I didn't tell her what Mr. Axelrod had said about my looking funny. While *funny* may be a bonus-plus in comedy acting, it is not necessarily the attraction that the greater Chicagoland population of guys is looking for. Otherwise, why hadn't they found me yet?

4

I heard the *click-clack-click* of dominoes and smelled the cigar smoke before I found Dad and Abuelo relaxing on the screened-in back porch. Afternoon sun shone on them. Beads of sweat blossomed in neat rows across their brows, undisturbed by the overhead fan. I sat down on our old refrigerator-sized what-color-is-it-anymore couch with the wobbly leg and balanced a Coke can on the wiggly arm. Our old furniture bands together out here like a neighboring tribe; that's why I like the porch. Familiar. Lived in.

But the domino board, atop an ancient folding card table, looked shiny new as usual. The ever-present cigar smoke has tinted the whole thing a mellow tobacco color, and every so often Dad gives it another coat of varnish. Dominoes littered the board, festive sandwiches of red and white, locked together with a gold pin at their centers. Black dots pocked their white faces, counting off in orderly patterns. These were no ordinary game pieces. Calling dominoes a game in our house is a joke.

Abuelo smashed the double-one tile onto the board. *"¡Tan!"* he whooped, beating the table with both palms, conga-style. "No ones, *eh?*" My grandfather, wiry, thin, and darker than Dad, is absolutely bald, and not because it's in style. He always wears the same thing: a boxy *guayabera* shirt, white today, with roses embroidered on the pockets, and the kind of thin dark pants that old people call trousers. Slippers at home, dress shoes when he goes out. Abuelo solved his fashion crisis long ago.

He waved his arms at my father. "You knock, then I knock, *¡tan-tan! como* Tito Puente." Neither of them had any ones in their hand to play.

Resolutely, Dad knocked twice, passing.

Abuelo cracked his knuckles down. "I win, for once, *¡Dios mío!*"

Dad exposed his remaining pieces to reveal several blanks, a low score. He reached over and spread out Abuelo's hand: twenty-six points. Dad just sat there, arms crossed in a yellow long-sleeved velour shirt, sweating and looking smugly across the table at his father.

Abuelo returned his gaze innocently. *"¿Qué?"* As if he couldn't add.

"Dame el dinero, Papito," Dad said. "Pay up!"

With lips tight, Abuelo opened a small leather coin purse,

plucked a dime from it, and tossed it onto Dad's side of the table. Quite a few dimes were stacked there, next to a cracked ashtray that said FONTAINEBLEAU HOTEL—MIAMI on it.

"Se acabó," muttered Abuelo. "I quit!" He winked at me and revealed the landscape of a grin he'd been hiding. He didn't really mind losing. *"A menos que . . . eh,* Violeta? Do you want to take my place?"

The game never stopped as long as another sucker came along.

"Sure, Abuelo," I said. "How're you feeling today?"

"Mucho mejor," he said, stubbing out what was left of his cigar and handing me his coin purse. *"¡Pero,* this *humedad!* It will kill me!" He fluffed his shirt up and down to get some air down the neck. Then he stepped back into the air-conditioned house.

A heat wave in September, and not even Indian summer yet. This didn't bode well for an early ski season.

"How was school today, Violeta?" Dad asked. I could barely hear him as we mixed the dominoes with our hands, the roar finally subsiding into distinct clicks as the tiles collided one last time, then came to rest.

"Good, I guess. I'm joining the speech team." I chose my ten pieces carefully from the blind pile, setting them upright horizontally. There are two schools on this; I prefer the low profile.

Dad stood his ten on end vertically. Maybe because he's so tall. Dad is six-two, with slightly olive skin that always looks tan, and black hair that's eroding in one small spot on top of his head. Besides the totally wrong shirt for a hot day, he wore polyester pants in a sickly watermelon color, leaving a good six inches of his ankles exposed. Green and white striped socks ran into his brand-new white bowling shoes with tassels on them, which he was breaking in by wearing around the house. I noticed he had fitted his cigar band around one finger as a ring. "Double nine!" he called. Highest double goes first.

I shook my head.

"Double eight!"

Still nothing.

"Double *siete!*" He ignored me and slapped down the double-seven piece.

I picked out the seven-five, one of two sevens in my hand.

"*Eh*speech, you say?" Dad remarked in a Spanglish accent. He must have been sitting out here with Abuelo for a long time. "There's a team for this?" He laid a piece down.

"Well, you've heard of debate, right, Dad? Tri-Dist doesn't have debate, but we do have these individual events that compete."

He nodded impatiently, waiting for my move. We each laid down a piece.

"Some events are like reading parts from a play, or reciting a famous speech. I'm doing Original Comedy; I'll have to write it myself." I looked at my hand, trying to decide, then went for the five-two.

Dad winced and knocked sharply on the domino board, passing.

Oh ho, no more sevens or fives in his hand already? My turn. I slapped the double-five piece at the end of the chain to form a T.

Dad had to knock again. "You have to write what your-self? Jokes?"

I nodded, laying down a tile. "My speech coach says I'm funny."

Dad sighed in relief and played a double. He took a happy puff from his cigar, pulled up a green and white striped sock, and fiddled with his cigar-wrapper ring. "But you come from a perfectly normal American household. What do you have to be funny about?"

"That's what I said." I kept a straight face, then hit him with a killer four-five, laying it off his double four slowly, to rub in the humiliation.

Dad took a domino from the spare pile, dropped it on its face, and spun it on its pinhead. He was getting nervous. But he played a low number from his hand.

"So, where will you get your material from?" he asked as I played off his blank. He scowled and knocked hard, once, passing.

Leda's invitation had given me an idea. "I thought maybe I could do something on a Cuban theme, but I'm not sure what. Could you help me?"

"There is nothing funny about Cuba," Dad said curtly.

"Oh, there must be something," I insisted.

"Sure," Dad exhaled, "if you think dictatorship is funny." He was still upset about having to pass. "Now are you going to play, Violeta?" he demanded.

I paused for effect, drew my weapon, and smacked the domino board with a nine-five, motioning for Dad to place it for me, since I couldn't quite reach the end of the chain in his corner. I donned Abuelo's innocent look. "Can you at least play off your double?"

He couldn't. I played my final two pieces and went out.

Dad knocked his dominoes faceup for me to see, shaking his head in disgust, and reached for a dime. I knew that, inside, he was marking this loss in his memory book of lifetime wins and losses. I smiled.

"There's nothing funny about this," Dad said grumpily just as Mom came out to the porch, carrying our toy poodle, Chucho, and the family calendar. "I quit. Will you put the dominoes away?"

"Aw, Dad, you didn't give me any ideas for my speech yet. And we only played one game."

"Maybe your mother has some ideas for the *eh*speech. But this game is over." He swept his dimes up from the corner of the domino board. "Unless..." He jingled his change at Mom. "Diane?"

Mom set Chucho down on the floor, where he immediately found Abuelo's discarded cigar wrapper and ate it. "I'll play," Mom said.

Dad gave her his handful of change, ground his cigar out in the ashtray, and retreated into the house.

★   ★   ★

Except for the extra legs and tail, Chucho looks exactly like a little old man who took a bath in superglue and rolled around on a hairdresser's floor. Dad inherited the dog from Madrina, his godmother, who had owned him as long as anyone could remember. Nobody knows Chucho's true age or agrees on what color he is for sure. He blends right in on the back porch.

As dogs go, he is more like a goat, which is why Abuelo calls him *cabrito* and Abuela puts her shoes up in the closet when she takes them off at our house. Chucho will eat anything, especially bits of things that look like they've been thrown away. Dad often wonders if Madrina ever fed the poor animal, but then I remind him that Chucho seems to be in the peak of health and, apparently, at least a century old. Whatever he's been eating, it agrees with him.

"Mom," I said as she settled with her calendar into Dad's old plaid overstuffed armchair, "Chucho just ate Abuelo's cigar band."

"Roughage," Mom replied, already turning the last game's pieces facedown and beginning to shuffle them. Chucho climbed up in Mom's lap and began gnawing on the family calendar. With any luck, he'd eat May.

We began another game.

"Mom," I said, hoping she was just distracted enough, "do I really have to go through with this *quince* party? I mean, is there any way we can just tell Abuela thanks, but no thanks?"

Unlike Dad, Mom will talk and pay attention to you while playing dominoes. She says it's because she's Polish and doesn't have the domino gene.

She looked at me, hurt, obviously not distracted enough. I could see foundations weaken and columns collapse in her mind as her plans were shaken. "You—you don't want to have the party?"

"No, no," I reassured her, "it's not that I don't *want* the party. . . . It's just not the kind of party kids have."

Mom let this sink in but didn't comprehend. "That's not what your *abuela* says."

"Well, she's from *Miami*," I said, as if it were Mars.

Mom still looked unconvinced.

"Look," I said, starting to feel desperate, "it's just not right for me. I mean, when's the last time I wore a dress?"

She surveyed her domino hand and laid a piece down. "There was that nice corduroy jumper I brought you from the shop," she suggested.

"That was fourth grade, Mom! And who would we even invite? I don't have enough cousins to fill a rental hall." Mom's family lives back East, in Pennsylvania, and we visited them; they never came to Chicago. And we didn't see much of Dad's relatives in the old neighborhood after Abuela and Abuelo left. Changing shifts at the pharmacy all the time made it hard for Dad to find two hours to drive out there and back, much less see anyone in between.

"There are friends . . . ," Mom said, probably meaning her old bowling-league buddies and the members of Mark's scout troop. As for my friends, I pretty much have hung out with Janell and Leda since my next-door neighbor moved away. "And won't it be great to see your cousins from the old neighborhood again?" she said.

I shrugged. We moved from the city to the house on Woodtree Lane when I was a baby. There wasn't a whole lot of old times' sake involved for me here.

"Mom," I said more insistently. "Look. I do not want to go out onstage, all dressed up, in front of people I hardly know, and talk about . . . about . . . being a woman." I looked her in the eye. "Would you?"

She thought about it for a second, then broke into a broad smile. "Why, I think that would be *lovely.* It's very nice of your grandmother to offer. Don't worry, we'll make sure you have a good time."

My heart sank. "I'm not wearing any pink dress," I said, sulking, as my grandmother came through the sliding door from the house. Chucho jumped off Mom's lap and walked a few rings around Abuela's stockinged ankles, making her pull her skirt close. She seated herself primly on the rickety old couch.

"*Oye,* Lupita," Mom said to her, "let's plan the dress shopping trip. We'll all three make a day of it!"

What a picnic that would be. I knocked on my turn and changed the subject. "Mom, Dad said you might be able to help me with this speech I have to write. I'm thinking of joining the speech team."

She nodded. "That sounds like a good idea. Some public speaking might be just the trick to get you onstage. What do you need to know?"

I gulped. "We're supposed to come up with an original theme, something no one else will think of. So I thought of doing some jokes about Cuba. You never hear much about Cuba."

Abuela sat up a little straighter and looked pained.

"How about dominoes?" Mom said. "The way your father plays is sometimes humorous."

I smirked and shook my head.

She won the hand by going out, and I handed her my dime.

"How about you, Abuela? Any ideas?"

"Me?" Abuela busily arranged her skirt. "No. *Yo no sé*," she demurred.

"Come on, Abuela," I said. "Help me. Tell me something about Cuba."

"Mmmm," she murmured, dipping her head, "this really is no *interesante . . .*"

"Come on, tell me something you remember from when you were growing up. It doesn't have to be funny. Please."

"Ah, *pues*, okay." A faint smile traced her lips. "Since you ask."

Her eyes glassed over, out to sea. "Was this lee-tle club, El Habano, *eh*? This place is my favorite. *Todo el mundo* would go in the summer each day for to *eh*swim, to eat lunch, to play the domino or cards. Sometimes would be a dance in the big ballroom. . . . *Ay*, the ballroom." Her voice grew stronger. "*Con cielos altos*, and many fountains, and the lights that hang . . . beautiful marble everywhere, and the *eh*spanish tiles on the floor. *Elegante*," she sighed. "Was a place *sin problemas*. Was our place."

Watching her, I saw it too. Saw how important it must have been to her.

"*Pero*, this Coo-ba is gone. *Muerta*," she said bitterly, the color draining from her cheeks.

The Communist revolution had taken all that away a long time ago. Abuela and Abuelo had been forced to leave the country. Whatever plans they'd had for themselves, just out of college, and for Dad, who was a baby, evaporated. They'd had to make a new life in the U.S., and then Luz came into the picture, and they'd moved up north to find work. They could never go back to what they'd had, I realized. All this resided in the diamond-edged look in Abuela's eye.

Mom asked smoothly, "Don't you and Teo belong to a new club, down in Mamita's neighborhood?" My grandparents moved back to Miami several years ago to be near Abuela's mother, who doesn't travel.

Abuela's face softened, but the hard look didn't leave her eye. "Is no the same," she said.

I guessed it wouldn't be. Maybe Dad was right. Maybe there is nothing funny about Cuba.

I gave up. "I've got homework," I said, reaching for the domino box. "Are you finished with these?"

Mom eyed Abuela, who shook her head and got up from the couch. Her color was returning. Only one thing could take my grandmother's mind off her troubles. A nice, friendly game of cutthroat.

"Juego," Abuela said, the corners of her mouth turning up. "I play now."

5

$\mathcal{F}$riday was a day off from school, so Abuela and Mom had me invite Janell and Leda dress shopping downtown with us. My two best friends had agreed to be *damas de honor,* part of my honor court.

"Whoever heard of a sweet fifteen party?" Janell said when I brought it up at lunch one day.

"It's *Cuban,*" I groaned. "Tradition with a capital 'T.' "

"I think it's excruciatingly cool," said Leda. "Mom wants me to have a ritual too. If I ever get my period." Leda, a year younger than Janell and me, had skipped eighth grade, or whatever they'd called it at her progressive school, and started as a freshman at Tri-Dist last term. Like

Janell and me, Leda had begged her parents to let her attend public high school. We had been three grade-school fish looking for a bigger pond.

By those standards, Tri-District High was a Great Lake, or a small sea: over five thousand students and faculty, known for a championship girls' basketball team, the TriJets; a losing football team, the Tridents; and our principal, Doc Waller, former Western B-movie costar and current record holder for growing Illinois's largest beet.

But even though I'd made some new friends over the past year, I still didn't know twenty-eight people I would ask to be in the court of such a strange personal event as this *quince* thing. Mom had found me a book through the Internet called *Quinceañero for the Gringo Dummy,* which explained all the elements of the traditional *quince* party. I scanned the first few paragraphs before tossing it in a corner of the kitchen. Basically, the *quince* is a show that opens with an entrance ceremony by the honor court, fourteen girls and fourteen guys, each couple representing a year, plus the fifteen-year-old herself, who has to give the first dance to her father. There's a cake, and music, and speech time—a lot like a wedding; I know, because I went to Janell's sister's reception.

We had to go shopping for dress ideas for me and the court members. So far, there were just the two of them. "Do I get to bring Willie?" Leda asked. Willie was her sometimes boyfriend who lived on the South Side, whom she'd met one weekend at a fur-awareness demonstration.

"Then who would I bring?" Janell wanted to know. My

friend since the first grade was not into dating, though I do remember her having a thing for Janet Conklin's brother back in 4-H. She says she has other pursuits right now, and we leave it at that.

"We're not doing escorts," I broke in. "Just like we're not doing a limousine arrival or a court of fourteen. You can bend some of the rules, according to Abuela." This had come as a relief to me, but it still wouldn't save me from the dreaded long dress. About that, she'd been adamant. I looked at Janell. "I wouldn't want to embarrass you. *I'm* the one being embarrassed that day."

★　　★　　★

Mom doesn't like driving in downtown Chicago, so we picked up Janell and Leda, locked the car at the C&NW station, and took the train to the Loop. I wore my favorite outfit, a suedelike tunic and loose pants in a very Septemberish rust color. I couldn't find my sandals before we left, so I had to wear red sneakers.

The others wore dresses; Leda and Janell must have tried on some formal wear in recent memory and knew the drill. When I first came out to the car, Mom and Abuela looked at each other and said something in Spanish; then Mom told me to go back inside and change into a skirt.

"You wear what you're going to try on," she said.

I muttered about not having anything but my old St. Edna's uniforms, so Abuela said, "Do you want borrow some-sing of mine, Violeta?"

Double the horror.

Go out in public in my grandmother's clothes? That'd

be like turning instantly old. I shuddered. "Let's just go," I said, getting in the car. I couldn't see what earthly difference changing would make. "We'll miss the train."

Abuela and Abuelo were right, September is one of the finest times to be alive in Chicago. The five of us emerged from the busy Canal Street station and walked east toward Lake Michigan. The stripe of water on the horizon was a deep, dizzy blue—the white dots on top of it, sailboats, and the white dots above those, seagulls. Warm, steady wind blew in off the lakefront, and the locust trees in Grant Park clung tightly to slightly yellow-tinged leaves.

We turned left, past a manic traffic cop, and followed Abuela up Michigan Avenue a couple of blocks to a bridal shop. CHEZ DOLL, read the discreet curlicue lettering on the window. We had to wait to be buzzed in through the front door.

"Who would hijack a wedding dress?" I asked. Then my surroundings awed me into silence.

The atmosphere inside was at once bustling and subdued. Mauve and gray walls met a silvery carpet as thick as the stacks of money the place must have been hauling in. Sales staff hurried to and fro beneath armloads of dresses. The well-turned-out clientele looked as though they'd gone shopping in order to shop here.

Our group of five stuck out like dandelions in a rose garden: Mom, sporting a snazzy yellow and green checked dress; Janell, matching the decor in a gray leotard and maroon wraparound skirt; Leda, with the peasant look; and me in my pant outfit and sneakers. Abuela presented a sober impression, except for her makeup, in a navy pleated skirt and white ruffly blouse. She was dressed exactly like the store clerks.

"Excuse me, ma'am. Do you have this in a size ten?" someone was already asking her.

We found our own clerk (though the card she gave us said SALES DELEGATE), and she abandoned us at the bridesmaids' section, a multicolored forest of satin, lace, and fibers unknown.

"Isn't this a little . . . formal?" I asked Abuela, pointing at a floor-length lacy, ruffly, pleaty thing in a honeydew shade.

Mom gave a whistle at the price tag. "Isn't it a little–expens-*ivo*?" she said, as though no one but us would understand Spanglish.

Abuela threw surreptitious glances over both shoulders. "*Sssst!* This is where we find *el modelo* for the dress! Then we have it copied by the dressmaker."

Mom gave her a sly nod.

"Cool!" said Leda.

"What are your colors?" Janell asked. "We'll be here all day if you don't narrow it down."

"Purple, not pink," I said, glancing at Mom. She and Abuela had given in to me on this one; we had decided last night.

"*Rosa,*" pouted Abuela, "is the *color tradicional* in our *familia. . . .*"

"It'll be sort of a pinky purple," Mom affirmed cheerily.

"Fuchsia," said Janell.

"Magenta," Leda added.

"Purple," I stressed. "It's my favorite color. But the *damas* dresses can be any color that looks good with it."

Abuela took charge again. "We choose your *vestido* first."

A squeal went up at the other end of the showroom, where a bride-to-be stood on a platform in front of her friends, the clerks, and the other customers to model the gown she was trying on. "I am not doing that," I stage-whispered fiercely in Mom's direction, but she was already engrossed in a purple and white pin-striped number.

I rolled my eyes at Leda. "Barney meets Wall Street," I muttered, brushing past to another rack. A shiny violet-blue gown drew my eye, but it had a plunging neckline. I don't even have a plunging neck.

Abuela sensed my interest and shook her finger at me. "The *chica* always wears many buttons in front." She fluttered her fingers in front of her chest to demonstrate.

"Like this?" asked Leda, displaying a long, bubble-gum pink, pearly, lacy dress that seemingly buttoned up to the nostrils, the neck was so high. "Looks like bat wings, doesn't it?" she said, pointing to the capelike collar.

I didn't see anything here that I might wear. My only criteria was: Would I, or would I not, bust out laughing when I saw my reflection in the mirror? Because if I couldn't carry it off in front of myself, I didn't see how I could get up in front of anyone else and dance the macarena with my dad. He swears that's the only dance he knows.

"I'll just wait in the dressing room," I sighed.

Abuela gave an evil grin. "You go," she said. "We bring. We bring."

★ ★ ★

The ugly truths one discovers about one's body while trying on clothes are best kept a secret, such as the stark blue vein in my left shoulder that looks terrible against spaghetti straps. But modesty was impossible.

Abuela, Mom, Janell, Leda, and our sales delegate, Iona, all trooped into the fitting room with me and at least two thousand purple dresses. Plus two pink ones that Abuela insisted I "just try."

Gaping into the full-length mirror, wearing the first gown, I discovered why clothing choice is important to a shopping trip. The summery dress Mom had picked out had a plum-colored bodice and a white muslin three-quarter-length skirt. In the harsh light of the dressing room, I—and everyone else, even though we *were* all girls—could see right through the skirt. I hadn't worn a slip, of course. And my athletic shoes gave me a macho air.

"Xena the Warrior Princess meets Tinkerbell," pronounced Leda.

"Try this one on," said Janell.

The saleswoman brought me a borrowed half-slip. I wriggled in and out of thousands of dresses, from those that would have been suitable for, say, a midsummer ship's christening to some that, I thought, would have been perfect for the funeral of the owner of a bridal shop.

"Shall we repair to the Bridal Circle?" Iona asked when I'd been zipped into yet another lavender chiffon. She wanted me to go out and model on the pedestal, where everyone else in the store was waiting for a good laugh, and subway lowlife probably pressed their noses up against the outside window for a free show whenever they passed this way.

"But we're all in here already," I pointed out, feeling a little punchy. Everyone else was looking strained too. "I've tried on so many dresses, I've got sliplash!" I said.

"Ha!" yelled Mom after a beat, followed by three silent *ha*s through open lips.

Iona was not amused.

"Hey," I said, grabbing one of my grandmother's peppermint ice cream selections. "Is this dress awfully pink, or is that just a pigment of my imagination?"

"HA!" Mom laughed more loudly, shaking her shoulders hard three times afterward.

Even Abuela smiled.

"If there won't be anything else . . ." Iona huffed from the room.

I got back into my comfy clothes, and we walked over to State Street to have lunch in the Oak Room at Marshall Field and Company.

6

The adults were arguing already. I hadn't been fifteen a week, and I could see that it was going to be a very long year.

After lunch, Mom and Abuela had reached an impasse in the clothing negotiations, nearly causing a scene in the After Five shop in Field's. Mom kept insisting on styles reminiscent of that fourth-grade corduroy jumper of mine, and Abuela couldn't stay away from the candy-frosting types. When the two appeared to be on the verge of a slap-fight, I reminded them that we had agreed the night before that I would have final say on the dress. I had worn Abuela down.

We marched back to Chez Doll and grabbed the first

purple and white dress I had tried on, plus a slip, which Mom charged to her credit card. The *damas* dresses would have to wait; no one complained about that. Luckily, the northbound train was crowded, so Mom and Abuela sat in separate rows all the way home. Janell and Leda looked relieved as we dropped them off, saying they'd see me tomorrow.

When we got home, Mom made me model the new dress for Dad and Abuelo. "But don't get it dirty, whatever you do!" she admonished. "We'll have to return it to the store after the dressmaker copies the pattern."

Dad must have asked in Spanish how much the dress cost. Mom said, "Nine ninety-five, plus tax," and Dad rolled his eyes and clucked his tongue. "But we'll get a refund," she assured him.

At dinner, Abuela had gone on and on about all the party pieces that needed to fall into place by May. "Here, in Lincoln Ville"—she insisted on saying the name as two separate places—"we arrange for the dresses, the hall, *la música, y las invitaciones. Por allá,* in Miami, I will find the party favors, the cushions for the gifts, and the *especial* guest book made to order. Then, don't forget—"

"And just who is supposed to pay for all this?" Dad asked.

Abuelo grinned. *"El papá."*

My brother, Mark, laughed with his mouth full and pointed at Dad.

"Y los padrinos," added Abuela seriously, "the *eh*sponsors who pledge to give one of these things as a gift to Violeta—to the *quinceañera.* Your *abuelo* will give the beegest gift," she pronounced, beaming, "for the hall."

Abuelo's smile vanished. Abuela said a few more words in Spanish to Dad.

"I am supposed to beg Carlos for *dinero*? No, not even for a *fotógrafo*, no." He listened to her for a moment, then sat back in his chair. "A photographer costs that much?"

"Claro que sí," murmured Abuela.

They continued their logistical discussion in Spanish, inflections and tempers rising and falling like stormy ocean waves. Mom and Abuelo joined the fray. Mark paid no attention. But I sat up straight when I started to hear *Violeta* over and over again, and *Dios,* which means God.

"What are you talking about?" I cut in.

Nobody answered.

"What are you saying?"

Dad's glare was all eyebrows. "Not now, Violet!"

I felt about five years old. "But I'm supposed to . . ."

They continued without me.

The rice I'd been eating stuck in my throat. This scene was too familiar. I slammed my fork down on my plate and got up. "You people are so rude!" I threw my napkin on the table. "It's not *my* fault I don't know Spanish. But then you wouldn't have your little code language, would you? How do you think that feels?"

"Don't you talk to your family that way!" said Dad.

Mom looked surprised to see me still there. "You may be excused, young lady," she said. Then she turned back to Abuela and finished what she'd been saying. *En español.*

★　★　★

Now my whole family was downstairs arguing. Urgent tones of Spanish drifted up to my room along with the too-sweet aroma of frying plantains for dessert. I don't like mushy ripe plantains anyway.

I flopped on my bed upstairs and coaxed Chucho into my lap. Even on a warm day, his poodle body heat was comforting. I kissed his neck and took a deep breath with my nose in his fur. Some dogs smell doggy, but Chucho, despite his other foul habits, always smells nice. Aromatherapy for the dog lover.

I popped a tape of mournful harmonica tunes into my cassette player and turned the volume low. "I've got the Cuban blues, Chucho," I told him. He sighed his little-old-man sigh and snuggled tighter into a ball on my lap.

I had finally blown up over something that had been boiling inside me for as long as I could remember. Mom and Dad had always used their shared language to discuss whatever they didn't want me and Mark to hear. Dad, of course, had grown up speaking Spanish. Mom had learned to speak it with the kitchen staff during her waitressing years in the city. That's what had endeared her to Abuela and Abuelo.

Spanish was currency. Currency I didn't have.

I understood a few dozen words, maybe more, now that I remembered Señora Wong's cognates. I could usually figure out what Mom and Dad were talking about from their tone of voice and the words I knew, but I couldn't connect those things to the whole Spanish vocabulary. "That must be how it sounds to a dog," I said to Chucho, who was snoring now. I thought of a comic strip I once saw about what dogs really hear when you talk to them: "Blah blah blah, Ginger, blah blah."

That's how I felt. Blah.

I couldn't see what the fuss was about—why I had to tip-toe around the subject. Abuela and Abuelo, Dad, and even Mom were so touchy about Cuba that anything I knew, I'd learned by accident. I was half afraid to ask pointed questions anymore, never knowing whether they would draw blood or be deflected like weak arrows with some offhand remark. Whichever it was, I rarely got answers.

Someone owed me an explanation. I decided to give my aunt Luz a call.

Chucho felt me stir and opened his big black eyes. He brayed a mighty yawn that ended in a little squeak, got up, and resettled himself on my pillow. I went to Mom and Dad's room to call Tía Luci long distance.

Dad's sister, Luz, is my favorite aunt. She lives on the West Coast and travels around the world, documenting whatever needs documenting with her camera. We never know when she's going to show up, but she always makes me feel like she came all the way just to see me. And she includes me in stuff no other grown-ups would.

Dad says she's *poca loca,* but I know he loves her and admires her. It's funny, though. Luz, who was born in Miami, seems more . . . Cuban than Dad. Or more willing to admit it.

"What's happening, Birthday Girl?" Tía asked when I reached her.

"Oh, I got in some trouble over this party Abuela wants me to have."

She purred sympathetically on the other end of the line.

45

"Tía Luci, did you ever have a *quince* party?"

"Not me, *niñita.* Your *abuelo* was too cheap," she said, kidding. "Actually, they gave me a trip to Spain for my fifteen. I refused the party."

"Refused!" God, Luz was a strong woman.

"I had already been to about fifty *quinces* back when we lived in Miami. All my Chicago friends were going to Spain. It was the cool thing to do. I leaned on Papi until he came around. It cost less than a party, that's for sure." She paused. "Mami, well, she was a different story. But Chicago wasn't Cuba, and it wasn't Miami either. I think she knew what I needed most. In the end, she let me choose."

"But what about the . . . the . . . *color tradicional*? You know, the pink dress?"

"Pink dress? It doesn't have to be pink anymore. Of course, Mami wore a pink dress. She made her *quince* in Cuba, you know."

Cuba. That *was* traditional. And not a subject I intended to broach downstairs.

"So," said Luz, "am I invited?"

"You'd come?" I asked.

"*Por supuesto.* I wouldn't miss your *quince* for the world!"

Well, that made one of us.

"You think it's a good idea, then?"

"I can't tell you what's on Mami's mind, but I'm sure her heart is in the right place."

I had known there wouldn't be any easy answers.

I sighed. "Thanks, Tía. Oh, one other thing. What is the tie-in with the church? That's what they're all downstairs arguing about right now. The truth is, we haven't all been to Mass together since Mark made his confirmation last spring. Will we have to do some kind of penance, or what?"

I heard the line hum while Tía Luci thought. I could almost see her roll her eyes and purse her lips before telling me, "Violet. How can you make your *quince* if you don't even know what it is? Would you jump out of a plane before looking for your parachute?" I could practically hear her smiling wryly. "Not everybody has a church ceremony, *chica.* Now go find out what you need to know before you start jumping off the big cliffs."

"I will, Tía. And thanks."

★   ★   ★

I marched back down to the kitchen to bust up the junta.

"I'm sorry I yelled at you," I began. "But I have something to say."

They all looked at me: Mom, perturbed; Abuela, skeptical; Abuelo, curious; and Dad, still upset, but looking sharp in a brown short-sleeved rib-knit shirt that zipped up the front. His long legs stuck out from under the kitchen table in knee-length blue plaid shorts. As a concession to the warm weather, he wore his bowling shoes with no socks.

Must I invite these people to my party? I thought, trying to hold firm. "Being the one turning fifteen and all," I said to my audience, "I just want to say that I would rather have gone on a trip to Spain. But I was not given that choice."

Abuela opened her mouth. *"However,"* I continued,

silencing her, "since my dear grandmother has offered to throw me a *quince* party, I have gratefully accepted the idea." If only to find out why, I thought.

Mom smiled and started to say something. *"Now,"* I went on, "I don't know what *Dios* has to do with it, but I do know one thing: The dress, the hall, the music, the photographs, the dinner . . . all this—*eh*stuff—is going to be a huge job to pull together."

Mom and Abuela heard this and nodded eagerly. Abuelo nodded soberly. At last, people were agreeing with me.

I continued. "As far as I can tell, it's going to take a no-holds-barred onslaught of time and energy from *all* of us. And not just the ladies." Here, I addressed Dad, who was squirming on the edge of his chair. "There will be tuxedos rented, friends invited, and dances learned."

I eyed each of them in turn. "And I'm making it my duty to see that every one of you"—I gave Dad an extra-hard stare—"looks presentable."

Dad started to protest, but I raised an index finger. "And we are going to have one person, and one person only, in charge: me! Is that clear?"

They looked at each other and buzzed worriedly.

"Listen up, people! This *quince* planning means war, and I need to know whose side you're on. Are you with me?"

Mom and Abuela nodded meekly.

Abuelo was unconvinced.

"Momentito, Violet!" said Dad. "That's fine to have one general, but don't forget, I have the keys to the war chest."

Mom stepped in. "She's right, though, Alberto. Too many generals spoil the troops." She raised an eyebrow, looking for any takers for her joke.

I ignored her. "Okay," I said. "Dad, you're general of finance. You'll have the final say on *el dinero*. Mom, you're captain of strategy, with Abuela and Abuelo as your Miami liaisons. Now, can everyone live with that?"

They hesitated, glancing at one another, then nodding.

"And you, Violeta. Who, may I ask, are you?" asked Abuelo, smiling his great piano-keyboard of a smile.

"That," I said, "is what we are about to find out." I picked up *Quinceañero for the Gringo Dummy* and retreated to my quarters.

7

I nearly fell asleep reading that night. The *quince* book must have been translated from the Spanglish; it was packed with information but pretty hard to follow. I read past the part I'd skimmed before.

After listing all the components of the traditional fifteenth-year celebration—the court, the formal wear, the dances—the book seemed to address me personally: "You may choses to embrace all of the elements of the *quinceañero,* or you may choses to flush traditions into the toilet and rewrite the ceremony for to fit your personality."

It was good to see this in writing. And, it turned out, the church service *was* optional.

This lightened my load a whole lot. I practically skipped down to breakfast to find Mom alone at the kitchen table, in an orange terry cloth robe and running shoes, writing.

"G'morning," I said, glancing at her work. Phew, no calendar today. I recognized the blue Snoopy notebook, open wide, with a floor plan on one page and her big loopy script covering the other. "Restaurant plans?"

Mom put down her Walgreens ballpoint pen. She never bought writing utensils but stocked up on freebies whenever she could get them. She looked at me, her wide face animated. "Violet, I think I've got it this time." She paused for suspense. "The two cuisines that I really know from top to bottom: Cuban and Polish. A combination that's never been tried before."

"That's for sure."

"Picture it," she said, framing the air with her hands. "The finest Polish and Cuban gourmet dishes in one restaurant. I call it: La Polka Grande!"

I smiled. Another of my mother's million-dollar ideas. "Polish meets Cuban in America. Sounds good to me," I said honestly. Mom's a great cook. I especially like the non-American dishes she makes. "But will it fly?"

Mom knit her brow and nodded slowly. "That is always the question."

It had been her dream since her waitressing days to open a restaurant, her own little neighborhood place that would serve great comfort food. She'd been saving her thrift-store earnings for years. Of course, the suburbs are teeming with ethnic places that serve soul food. But Mom was determined to find her niche. Someday.

I whipped up my own breakfast, a dish I like to call Cornflakes and Milk, and sat down at the table with her.

I love our kitchen. The built-in cabinets are made of real wood, with a pretty grain the color of maple syrup. Very breakfasty. Of course, nothing else matches them. The oval kitchen table has a fake-marble top and four fake-stone columns for legs. Five of the chairs are yellow vinyl (finds at the Rise & Walk), but the sixth is a black ladder-back wooden model that Mark and I dubbed the Death Throne. One of us is forced to use it whenever Abuela and Abuelo come to visit. Shiny red paper scattered with little gold fleurs-de-lis wraps the walls, and the floor is done up in indoor/outdoor carpet in a blue-green shade not found in nature.

Mom's thrift-store discoveries hang everywhere. My favorites are the gold, plaster-of-paris, smiling and frowning Janus masks; a wrought-iron wall clock in the shape of a chicken that always says 5:30; a framed, signed portrait of Betty Crocker; and a goofy plaque with loud lettering that reads WORLD'S GREATEST KNITTER. No one can say Mom doesn't have an eye for Americana. She collected it all to decorate her someday restaurant. Incredibly, this stuff is back in style now.

"Mom, can I talk to you about the party? We're supposed to pick a theme."

She closed her notebook. "The party is my top priority, sir!" she said, snapping off a salute and smiling.

I grinned back through my cornflakes. It was too bad I'd been so rough on my family the night before, but it'd had to be done.

I swallowed. "That book you gave me says you don't have to follow traditions to the letter. You can go with whatever's right for you. I heard the same thing from Abuela and Tía Luci. So we don't have to do anything we don't want to."

She listened.

"The book says there are places that will coordinate the whole party for you, all the stuff: banquet hall, catering, invitations, music—the works."

She nodded. "Lupita did mention that. It sounds so impersonal, though."

"But then there won't be so many arguments. It'll be a package deal." I desperately wanted out of the decision-making game. I might have pulled off my coup the night before at the kitchen table, but I knew my powers would fade when it came down to the nitty-gritty. And I understood one thing: This *quinceañero* had to make me look good because, what with the pictures and all, people were going to remember it for a long time.

"We'll check into it. Now, what about your theme?"

The Janus masks had inspired me. "How about 'All the World's a Stage'? Since I'm going to be in the spotlight."

She considered. "I love it!" she said, smiling. "We can get a real spotlight."

"And hundreds of little tiny white Christmas lights, hanging from the ceiling."

"And one of those disco balls."

"Easy, Mom. Elegant. Think elegant." I'd have to watch like a hawk to keep her and the others in line. "We need a new notebook for the party plans," I said. "And a better calendar. The book says you've got to keep it all in one place. 'One places,' it says."

"Party Central." Mom nodded. "I'll look for something at the drugstore today."

★　★　★

Mom drove Leda and me to school for our meeting on her way to the store. Janell came straight from ballet class. She met us, still in her layered dance clothes, in Room C206, home of the Tri-Dist speech team. The jaundiced walls of the oversized room whispered with anticipation. Older kids, juniors and seniors whom I didn't know, leapt among the tiered desks, reciting lines and high-fiving their friends. I suddenly wanted to be one of them.

Leda, demure today in an Indian cotton shirt and jeans, rolled her eyes at me. "Puh-lease," she said. "Is this Overacting 101?"

I pretended to swoon. "Intro to Melodrama." But inside, I was salivating.

A sophomore named Gina, whom I knew from gym period, smiled my way and passed us some handouts headlined COMPETITION CHOICES. Janell, her sleek cap of dark brown hair pinned up in a facsimile of a bun, scanned the page and frowned. "This stuff all looks okay to me. Why do I have to be the one to do poetry?"

"Ask not for whom the bell tolls . . . ," cracked Leda in a quavery voice.

"Hey, look, Janell." I waved my copy of the handout at her. "It says *choices*."

"Tell that to The Ax," she said.

54

Leda patted her shoulder. "Maybe I can talk to him for you. Get you into . . . Extemporaneous Speaking. Or how about this one: Radio? Don't worry. I've got some clout."

Janell and I exchanged looks. Funny, she probably did have some clout. Leda always managed to slither her way behind the scenes.

Now Ms. Joyner stood on the practice stage down front. "People! People, let's get started. I do have a life, let's get on with the show." Kids scrambled for seats. "I'm Tracy Joyner. And this is John Soloman," she said, introducing a short, slightly pudgy teacher with a ruddy face, bowl haircut, and brown plastic-rimmed glasses that masked his eyes.

"Where's The Ax?" I wondered aloud.

A tall, quiet-looking guy in a Michael Jordan T-shirt and shorts a couple of seats over caught my eye. Softly he said, "Mr. Axelrod—he never comes down for this kind of thing."

I shrugged at him.

Then the house lights, the fluorescents in the ceiling fixtures that resembled giant ice cube trays, dimmed. A single spot came up on Ms. Joyner. Her pause filled the atmosphere, and she made eye contact with her audience. "Welcome, speechies," she said powerfully. "You are all here because you have talent."

Leda jabbed me in the ribs with an extra-bony elbow.

Ms. Joyner went on. "I am glad to see so many familiar faces. Most of you already know how speech competition works. For the rest of you, this will be an introduction to the different individual events. We'll talk about selecting material and competing in tournaments at another time." She hesitated and stared past us, out over our heads. "Rick? Do you have anything to add?"

That had to be The Ax. But if he wasn't down here, where was he?

The puffy sound that comes from someone touching a live microphone punctuated the air. Overriding the static in an invisible sound system, a deep, none-too-jovial voice boomed: "Ladies and gentlemen, some statistics: We have among us five graduating seniors, four experienced juniors, and several promising new members. This is the year we take State! But—" He arrested a hurrah.

Everyone sat motionless on the edge of their seats. You could've heard a butterfly hiccup.

"Remember, we have only two rules on this team: Practice like crazy. And kick ass!"

The room erupted into well-enunciated cheers.

This, I thought, was going to be interesting.

8

*R*ick Axelrod, department head by day, legendary speech coach by night (and weekends), likes to direct team meetings and practice sessions from the lighting booth, where junior techies learn to run lights and sound for theater productions. This gives The Ax absolute authority, or so Clarence Williams, the soft-spoken guy who'd answered me before, told me as Ms. Joyner tried to restore peace to the room by threatening us with a prop saber.

Clarence didn't seem to mind Mr. Axelrod's arrogance. "The truth is," he said, sliding into the empty seat next to me, "The Ax is the greatest coach this district—and maybe the state—has ever known. You'll see," he added, caramel-colored eyes reflecting an inner grin. I studied him further. His buzz-cut hair was dusty brown, and black-rimmed glasses framed an angular face with a deep bronze cast.

I smiled back.

Ms. Joyner menaced us one last time with the rubber sword, and the house lights went out.

In the darkness, the disembodied voice of The Ax called over the mike: "Zeno Clark. Dramatic Interpretation. You're on."

The stage spot came up on a lone male, one Zeno Clark, presumably. His straight brown hair tapered to his shoulders, and his slim frame swam in loose jeans and an oversized T-shirt. He placed his hands behind his back in a practiced manner and hung his head.

Was this some kind of punishment? For him, or for us?

Slowly, he raised his head and met the audience with his eyes. Any awkwardness vanished. Zeno Clark, or whoever he was now, exuded what could only be described as a presence.

His gaze slid to a point somewhere above our heads and then he began, in character, " 'In my younger and more vulnerable years, my father gave me some advice that I've been turning over in my mind ever since.' " He cocked his head and shifted his focus to another point in space. A half octave lower, he said, " 'Whenever you feel like criticizing anyone, just remember that all the people in this world haven't had the advantages you've had.' "

Zeno returned to the first voice. " 'In consequence, I'm inclined to reserve all judgments.' "

He paused.

" 'Only Gatsby was exempt from my reaction–Gatsby,' " he said with a sudden, visceral bitterness, " 'who represented everything for which I have an unaffected scorn.

" 'But there *was* something gorgeous about him,' " the character admitted. " 'His was an extraordinary gift for hope,' " and here Zeno's voice quivered, " 'a romantic readiness such as I have never found in any other person and which it is not likely I shall ever find again.

" 'No–Gatsby turned out all right at the end.' " Zeno flashed his eyes. " 'It is what *preyed* on Gatsby, what foul dust floated in the wake of his dreams . . .' " He slowly dropped his head to his chest for a moment, before falling out of character and regaining his own body posture.

"What preyed on Gatsby," said Zeno more intimately, making eye contact with us again, "was the past. In this dramatic interpretation, narrator Nick Carraway observes one man's futile attempt to recapture the glory of youth and love in *The Great Gatsby,* by F. Scott Fitzgerald."

Zeno repeated the transformation and went on, in the voice of Nick Carraway, about his neighbor Jay Gatsby, a rich man obsessed with reclaiming his old love, Nick's cousin Daisy. When a new character spoke, Zeno shifted his weight, changed his tone, and moved his gaze to a different spot in the darkened room.

I felt like a theatergoing Jonah swallowed by the whale–the story *engulfed* me.

Nick said, " 'Gatsby wanted nothing less of Daisy than that she should go to Tom and say: "I never loved you." I said to him, "I wouldn't ask too much of her. You can't repeat the past." ' "

Gatsby answered, incredulous: " 'Can't repeat the past? Of course you can!' "

For some reason, I found myself thinking of Abuela.

The whole audience knew it was never going to work. After Gatsby's inevitable downfall, Nick found himself caught up in the same trap. " 'So we beat on,' " Nick said, arms outstretched, " 'boats against the current, borne back ceaselessly into the past.' "

Zeno dropped his eyes and placed his hands behind his back, and the stage went black.

★   ★   ★

Two things were true when the house lights came back up to applause: I was thoroughly, with every cell of my body and every deep well of my soul, in love with Jay Gatsby, Zeno Clark, and the theater. Also, Clarence Williams was looking at me.

On my right, Leda and Janell were talking to someone else they knew, expressing the awesomeness of Zeno's performance. I slid my eyes back at Clarence, who still looked at me with that knowing smile, waiting. "Well?" he demanded, as if he had coached Zeno himself.

"In-incredible," I sputtered.

Clarence nodded smugly. "He took State last year in Dramatic Interp, only a junior. The Ax was his coach."

I whistled in awe. This got Leda's and Janell's attention, and I introduced them to Clarence.

"You know an awful lot about the team," I said to him. "Are you a senior?"

He smiled modestly and pushed his glasses up on his nose. "Hardly. I'm a freshman. All my brothers were

Extempers. I tagged along for years. I feel like I practically own the event."

"Brothers, eh?" said Leda.

Janell looked impressed. "Extemporaneous Speaking–that's the toughest, I heard. Don't you just make speeches up on the spot, in front of the judges?"

"There's more to it than that," Clarence said. "We draw topics and then build an argument. You have to be up on history and current events. There's lots of prep work."

Again, Ms. Joyner touchéed us from the stage with her fake sword, cutting off the conversation. "We have ten more events to get through, gang. Don't make me commit hara-kiri!" She gave us the old impaled-through-the-armpit gag and turned the stage over to the next speaker.

We made it through eleven performances, including one girl who read a radio newscast, complete with weather and advertisements, and one unlikely-looking pimply white guy who gave a burning rendition of Martin Luther King Jr.'s "I Have a Dream" speech. Then The Ax let us go.

"You've each been assigned a coach," Mr. Axelrod's amplified voice informed us. "Check the bulletin board on your way out."

I'd been assigned the "humorous" coach, Mr. Soloman, with an appointment after school the following Wednesday. That was my piano lesson day. I caught up with Mr. Soloman on his way out and told him I'd have to switch times with somebody.

"Who's on first?" he asked.

"What?"

"No, What's on second, Who's on first!" He winked. "Gotcha!" He shook my hand and said we'd get started on Tuesday, then. "What topic do you want to write about?"

"I don't know," I said.

"I Don't Know's on third," he said, and winked again. "See you Tuesday."

9

I barely had time to finish all my homework that weekend. Saturday got kind of busy after dinner, when Dad and I trounced Mom and Abuelo in team dominoes after a lengthy match/rematch syndrome that nobody wanted to end. Abuela came out to kibitz during the commercials of the Spanish television miniseries she was watching, *El Amor y Almuerzo.*

"*Love and Lunch?*" I said. "What kind of show is that?"

Abuela scrunched up her face, cracking the thick whitish-pink lipstick she'd applied with a steamroller. "No love and lunch," she said. She began to try to explain, then shook her head. "These things, they do not translate literal-*mente.*"

And Sunday we all drove to the old neighborhood to go to twelve o'clock Mass. This seemed to take all day, because Abuela and Abuelo stopped to chat with a few hundred of their old friends out on the church steps afterward.

St. Ignacio's is nothing like St. Edna's, our sleek, modern church in the suburbs. At St. Edna's, the furnishings are so spare that the stations of the cross look like the universal symbols on rest rooms and road signs. St. Ignacio's, on the other hand, was built a hundred years ago, when Catholics still believed in pumping up the decor to inspire the proper state of awe.

The building itself is made of huge limestone blocks set stories high, broken by vaulted archways of heavy honey-colored wood at every door and window. Wide concrete stairs frame the church on all sides, and an old-fashioned copper-tipped steeple, the metal long gone to sea green, tops it off. Tiny first-floor windows shine a deep amber, etched in a crisscross pattern, and a rainbow of stained glass forms starburst designs around ornamental crucifixes in the large panes overhead. Personally, I wouldn't mind visiting St. Ignacio's more than just a couple of times a year.

Inside, hundreds of votive candles flicker from orange glass holders in little alcoves set with kneelers. Rows of maple pews face a high stage that houses the altar and organ. The loft above them holds a choir balcony. The way it's cut out of the wall reminds me of a puppet theater. St. Edna's doesn't have a stage for its altar, much less a loft, choir, or puppet theater. We are supposed to focus on the priest, and therefore on God. I couldn't help thinking that if God had a flair for the dramatic, as all accounts suggested, he'd probably like St. Ignacio's better.

Out on the steps, my brother, Mark, practiced his pitching windup while I trailed after Mom and Dad, who were saying hello to people they knew. A man about Dad's age, huskier and with more dark hair, approached, shook Dad's hand, then grabbed him in a bear hug.

"Berto Paz, *¿cómo estás?*"

"*Quién* . . . Rudi? Rudi García, is that you?"

They danced around a minute; then the man released my father. "This is Rudi García, everybody. Diane, Violet," he presented us. "Mark," he said uncertainly, looking over a shoulder; then he spied Mark's blue Cubs hat a ways away and pointed him out. "Rudi and I grew up on the same block. He moved away when we were teenagers. What are you doing back in the old neighborhood, *amigo?*"

"You know what? I got tired of L.A. It's no place to raise four daughters. Too many movie stars, no?" Rudi smiled, his round cheeks pushing laughter right up into his dark brown eyes. "So this is your Violet," he said. "I hear you are making your *quinceañero.* Congratulations!" To Dad and Mom, he said, "You must be very proud."

"Proud?" Dad's olive skin ripened a shade, and he tried to cover with a goofy smile.

Mom came to the rescue. "Oh, we are *very* proud. Violet turned fifteen this month, but the celebration is in May. You'll come, won't you? And bring your family."

Rudi nodded. He clapped a hand on Dad's shoulder. "Put me down for some of the refreshments, *amiguito.* Send me a bill." He leaned over to give Mom and me a kiss on the cheek. "It was nice meeting you! Call me sometime, Berto." They shook hands again, and he left.

"You and Rudi grew up together, huh, Dad?" I said. Why was that so hard to picture? "When's the last time you saw him?"

My father did some inner calculation. "Oh, it's been at least twenty, twenty-five years. That Rudi! You know what he did one time . . . ?"

I wasn't listening. A guy my dad hadn't seen in twenty years had just offered to pay for refreshments at my party. That was like signing your paycheck over to someone you met at the bus stop who'd been kind enough to tell you your bus had gone by. Who was that generous?

Rudi García, obviously. Mom was already making a note on the back of the church bulletin with one of the dozen Chestnut Oaks Golf Course pencils she carried in her purse. "Give this to your *abuela,* Violet," she said. Abuela was keeping track of sponsors for the party. "And tell her it's time to go!"

We drove by White Castle for lunch on our way home, where Mark made a pig of himself as usual, ordering a whole dozen Slyders but eating only nine and a half. We finished the leftovers in the car.

"*Ay,* I am going to miss the White *Castillo,*" Abuelo declared sadly, crossing his arms over his peach-colored *guayabera.* He'd be going home in a week or so, and the hamburger chain didn't operate in Miami.

"We'll send you some frozen ones, don't worry," Mom said.

At that, Abuelo displayed several octaves of teeth and

practiced a drumroll on his knees. I would miss him when he went home.

★ ★ ★

I changed into jeans and watched the end of a late-season Cubs game on TV with Mark (Cubs beat the stinky Mets at Wrigley, 5–3). Then I helped Abuela make Cuban chicken salad for a light dinner. She always lets me decorate the top with baby peas and pimientos. Maybe I'm getting too old for that, but there's something satisfying about making art out of vegetables. That's why the guy who invented Mr. Potato Head did so well, no doubt.

After dinner, which we all picked at, someone said the word *domino,* and I saw a blood lust surface in Dad's eyes.

Mom squinted and returned his gaze. "Rematch?"

Abuelo was already jingling the change in his pocket for dimes (he can find them without looking), and Abuela rubbed her manicured hands together greedily.

"Count me in!" I said. "Do you have any dimes, Mom?"

"Not for you, young lady. These dishes need to be washed, and then homework."

"Dishes? But what about Mark . . . ?"

The four adults headed for the back porch, Abuelo stopping to pull two cigars from the fridge. Mark pushed up from the table and ran.

★ ★ ★

I had just finished my workbook assignment for Spanish class when Dad knocked his brisk domino knock on my door and walked in.

I put down my pencil. "What happened to you?"

"Kicked out of the game for cheating," he said, with a

67

hint of a grin. "No, I'm working the early shift tomorrow, and I want to get some reading done. So I thought I'd say good night." He sat down on my bed and crossed his legs in their burnt-orange polyester slacks, with no intention of leaving. Sometimes when Dad wants to talk, you have to worm it out of him.

I took the bait. "What is it you're reading?"

"*¡Ay, caramba!* Your *abuela* thinks I should read up on this *quinceañero* business. And since I'll be paying for it . . . I thought I should see if there's a financial section. A big party is a big expense, and . . ."

I narrowed my eyes. Dad was never this talkative about money. "You'll have lots of help paying for it," I said. "Dad, how come you act like you don't know about the *quinces*? You must've gone to some, growing up in the old neighborhood, or when you lived in Miami."

He gave me the same goofy smile he'd used on his friend Rudi earlier. "I wouldn't do it," he admitted. "Some of the kids I ran around with thought it was—*afeminado*—to be in a court. To have to dress up in a monkey suit, and learn all those silly dances . . . we just wanted to be Americans, to drive around in cars and be cool."

"And you still can't dance to this day."

He threw me a look of mock hurt. "I can dance the macarena!"

I didn't have the heart to tell him how uncool the macarena was.

"But your friend Rudi—he did go to the parties, didn't he?"

Dad ducked his head. "Well, yes, apparently so."

Aha!

"And you're *jealous* of your old pal for knowing more about your own daughter's *quince* than you do!"

Dad's face sort of melted then, his features becoming fluid in a way that signaled my cross-examination had worked. I thought about what I had just said. "That's okay, Dad," I soothed him. "I'd never even heard about this *quince* thing before Abuela brought it up. I don't know any more than you do, other than what I've read in this book." I patted the copy of *Quinceañero for the Gringo Dummy* on my desk.

"Er, that's what I've come to ask you, Violet. Can I borrow that book for a day or two?"

Oh no you don't, I thought. The book was the only thing that stood between me and complete chaos. "Why don't you just ask Abuela if you have questions?"

He stood to leave and growled, "She's the one who told me to go read the book! Said if I wasn't paying attention to the world around me when I was growing up, well, it wasn't her fault."

We both gave fractured smiles.

"So can I borrow it, please?" Dad asked. "I'll make it worth your while." He pulled a cassette tape from the pocket of his shirt and tossed it on the bed. It was his favorite *Women in Blues* compilation tape, the one with Koko Taylor singing "Hound Dog" on it. I'd been begging him to make me a copy of it forever.

I handed over the book. "Deal."

10

The *quince* bible was making the rounds. "Listen, listen. Get this," Leda said to Janell and me a few days later. She sprawled on my bed in jeans and a tank top that said HERBIVORE on it, paging through the manual. "After the opening dance number by the court comes the presentation—when the *quince*-babe makes her entrance. That's you, Violet," she reminded me, as if I needed it. "Followed directly by the waltz with the father."

I grimaced.

She quoted from the book: " 'The presentation shows the passage from the girl onto a woman.' "

Janell hooted. "Sounds suggestive."

"It says that different countries have different customs. In Puerto Rico and Mexico the *quince*-chick makes her entrance and sits on a throne, where one of her parents changes her shoes from flats to heels. You don't even own a pair of heels, do you?"

"Dad says they're bad for your feet."

"Oh, come on," said Janell. "So are toe shoes." She sat on my floor in tan leggings and an orange T-shirt, stretching. "What's wrong with dressing up every once in a while?"

My face colored. "Sometimes you just have to make your own style," I said. Thank God for Mom's common-sense approach to fashion.

"Listen, listen," Leda interrupted, and read aloud: " 'Cuban *quinceañeros* lies somewhere in between the myth and the legend. Girls has been presented in giant silver teacups, in swings lowered from the ceiling, and on an Egyptian litter carried by bearers in costume.' " She turned her blue eyes pleadingly on me. "*Dude . . .* can we?"

"I'm not that much of a ham. Besides, the theme's not Egyptian."

" 'All the World's a Stage,' " said Janell. "I like it. So, the presentation has to be dramatic."

"Hey! I know. You could descend from a spiral staircase in one of those vamp outfits," suggested Leda.

The thought made me squeamish. "That'll all be taken care of." I waved a hand to dismiss the subject. "We're going to a party planner who will design the whole event. We'll have rehearsals and everything. There are supposed to be some dances. I'll let you guys know when the parts have been figured out."

"But we'll definitely perform, right?" asked Leda. "One of the big production numbers or something?" She *was* that big of a ham.

"This isn't a Broadway show," I said.

Janell looked at me like lightning had just struck. "But it could be. It could be," she said excitedly. "We could give performances instead of going through those old-fashioned routines. I could give my poetry interpretation and do one of the jazz numbers from last year's recital. Then Leda could do"– she gazed at our friend quizzically–"whatever it is that Leda is doing, and you could be the star attraction."

Leda leaned forward, intrigued.

"It sounds like fun, but there are these traditions–"

Leda jabbed a finger at the book. "But it says right here that you can throw tradition in the toilet and flush hard, if you want."

Janell nodded. "Yeah, why should you follow a tradition that doesn't reflect who you are? You've already decided on an all-girl court. Why can't you take that a step farther?"

I shook my head. "All-girl courts have been done. You don't understand, Abuela has already made the appointment with Señora Flora. Party planner to the *eh*stars."

"Party planner to the stars?" crowed Leda.

I wasn't sure I believed this anymore, but I said, "It'll be easier this way. Less decisions. Less arguments."

They looked at me. "Between them, not us," Janell concluded.

It appeared that I was going to have to please everybody. "Look," I said. "As far as I'm concerned, you guys are the most important ones in this production. Well, besides my dad. And me."

"Yeah, and you," echoed Leda with a note of jealousy.

"Honest. I'll take any suggestions that you have and refer them to the committee. You guys are my *damas*. They'll have to listen to you." I folded my arms.

This seemed to satisfy them for the time being. Janell turned to a stack of poetry books she'd brought with her, and Leda and I quizzed each other on Spanish vocabulary for a while. We seemed to do more harm than good.

"Window?" Leda asked.

"Ventana," I answered.

"No, that's French. The *español* is *fenêtre*."

"No, it's not," I argued. "*Fenêtre* is French."

She looked at me, confused. "What is it again?"

By the time we'd both made it through the list, I knew we were doomed. The test was tomorrow.

Janell got fed up with our bickering. "Why don't you just ask your dad to coach you?" she asked me.

This hadn't even occurred to me. "We don't . . . speak Spanish together," I said. "Mom says she can't help because she learned by ear. And Abuela tried to teach me and Mark one time, but it didn't work out."

"So what happened?" asked Janell.

"Not much. Before Abuela and Abuelo moved back to Miami, Abuela brought some Spanish workbooks over. She tried to hold a little class. *'Es una lástima,'* she said, *'que no hablan el español.'* Mark and I didn't pay much attention. It was the weekend, and we wanted to be playing." I sighed. "I guess I'll just have to study some more tonight."

Leda stuck her notebook back in her rainbow-colored backpack. "Aren't we gonna look at Janell's stuff?"

"Sure. What've you got so far?" I said, moving over to Janell's spot on the floor. Leda joined us.

"Well, I've got it narrowed down to Maya Angelou and Alice Walker, but I need one more poet. And a theme. I'm supposed to pick several poems that demonstrate one concept."

"Who's your coach?" Leda asked.

"I've got Ms. Joyner."

"I've got that new guy, Mr. Soloman," I put in. "Who's your coach, Leed?"

"Mr. Axelrod," she said casually.

"No way!" said Janell, catching my eye. How did Leda do it? I shrugged.

Leda tucked stray strands of her long white-gold hair behind her ears. "Yeah, well, Rick doesn't usually coach Oratory, but he said he had an opening for a sophomore."

Rick? This was too much. "I'm going to tell him that you're only fourteen!" I threatened. "That you're a sophomore in name only. You should still be buying elevator passes and paying cafeteria tolls with the freshmen."

Leda stuck her tongue out at me. "I got here fair and square," she sassed. "I can't help it if I'm gifted."

"We'll see how gifted you are when the competition starts," Janell said, stuffing her books in her dance bag. "I'm going to go get in some horn practice before dinner." She got up. "You guys have been a real big help. Looks like I've got some more reading to do before I can pick my routine." She looked at us sympathetically. "I'm glad I don't have to *write* it."

"Hey, are you coming over this weekend?" I asked. It was party time at the Paz house. Abuela and Abuelo had invited all their old friends over for a domino marathon. Dad was moving the extra back-porch furniture out to the garage to make way for more playing tables, and Mom was already cooking. People would come and go all weekend, and the domino matches would never end.

"Can't," said Janell. "We're visiting my cousins in Kankakee."

"I'll be there for some of it," said Leda. "I can practice my Spanish on your relatives. But on both days we're collecting donations for a homeless shelter. Beth signed us up for six suburbs. I'll probably still be out there Sunday night, canvassing in one of those coal miner's hats with a flashlight on it, trying to make quota!"

"Jeez," I said. "I thought they were going to lay off."

She shuddered. "Speech team can't start soon enough for me."

"First tournament's in three weeks," I said. "Hang in there."

11

Señora Wong impaled us with the vocab test. She made us fill in the blanks in a paragraph with nouns we were supposed to know, and write out complete sentences using forms of suddenly unfamiliar verbs. Howls of anguish erupted when kids saw that memorizing the word list wasn't going to cut it.

"We are supposed to be learning to *eh*speak *el español,*" said the ruthless Señora Doble-U, who claimed to have learned the language as an exchange student in Mexico. "Do you expect *el presidente de España* to fax you the vocabulary for your interview when you are big *reporteros* for the *Tribune?*" This class was beginning to sound like my house.

Afterward, a solemn Leda low-fived me on the way out the door, wishing me a *bueno jour.*

Things improved later in the day in Ms. Joyner's class, as usual, when we got to watch a video of Richard Nixon's famous televised "Checkers" speech. Checkers was this cocker spaniel that some dude in Texas sent Nixon, and Nixon's kids fell in love with the dog. In answer to rumors of a campaign slush fund and in the interest of full disclosure, "Tricky Dicky" informed the American people that, concerning Checkers, "regardless of what they say about it, we are going to keep it."

I sort of liked the guy for that, until he came to the end of his speech. He said that no matter what people said about him, he was going to keep fighting, "until we drive the crooks and Communists . . . out of Washington." Like he should talk.

I knew that Cuba had been forced into Communist rule when Fidel Castro took over. Now, it seemed, there was Communism where, before, there had been people. I couldn't connect the two. To me, Communism was this mean junkyard dog I'd never had any personal quarrel with but that had bitten others one too many times. It was the reason I'd never seen the town in Cuba where my dad was born; that was the only bone I had to pick with it. Say the word at home, though, and I'd get an earful about *socialismo* in Spanish or the Russian occupation of Poland in English, depending on which parent was around. Mom and Dad seemed to share Nixon's view: all Commies are bad.

But maybe not all of them believed in the government. Probably only some did, and the rest just had to pretend. I bet that's hard.

The unstable horizontal hold on the video chopped Nixon's fuzzy outline into a dozen pieces. "Can you believe how crappy TV reception was back then?" Janell whispered.

I nodded soberly, as though I'd been tracking it since. "I don't think cable would've saved him, though."

Afterward, Ms. Joyner launched into a soliloquy about the power of persuasive speech that was quite convincing in itself. She persuaded me that maybe I could somehow persuade Señora Wong to let me take the vocabulary test over again. I might invite her to the domino party this weekend, let her win a few dimes. Let her take Chucho home, like some Cuban "Checkers" bribe.

But there were pitfalls to persuasion. "Look what happened to Socrates," Ms. Joyner pointed out. Socrates was forced to drink a cup of poison hemlock when his speeches threatened to put his fellow philosophers out of business.

Hmmm. Perhaps I would leave Señora Wong alone and my Spanish grade up to fate.

★   ★   ★

Later that day, after classes, I headed for the speech office in C building to keep my appointment with Mr. Soloman. I felt sorry for kids who had lockers in this wing; they were always having to run to class. They hung around leisurely now after the last bell, savoring the moment, chattering and shouting and slamming metal doors. My eyes brushed over them like a minesweeper, searching for The Ax so he couldn't sneak up on me. But neither he nor Mr. Soloman was at large in the halls or the speech office, which was empty, the door invitingly ajar.

I walked in. The only chair-desks had been pushed

down the corridor, so I sat at Mr. Axelrod's desk and let my pack slide to the floor at my feet. I also let my guard down a hair.

The Ax kept a tidy desk, everything arranged carefully on one of those big square blotter things for writing. He could've made it through the express lane at the supermarket with eight items or less: one half-empty plastic bottle of springwater, capped; stack of permission slips for some speech-related trip, signed; felt pen, capped; magnetic paper-clip holder, full; stapler, probably ditto; calendar set made of plastic cubes you had to turn to the right date, today showing; and a five-by-seven photograph of a dark-haired, alabaster-skinned woman, laughing, in a simple, chrome-plate frame: the mysterious Mrs. Ax, killed, so they say, in a car accident the night after their wedding.

She looked so alive in the photo.

The bottom desk drawer was open a crack, so I pushed it closed, then, curious, opened it again. A stack of yellowed *Variety* newspapers. A beat-up *Our Town* script. I pushed these aside and spied an envelope marked LETTERS in a strong, gruff hand.

Letters? From his wife?

Then a strong, gruff voice shook me. "Ms. Paz!"

I froze in horror—The Ax himself loomed over me, dressed for a funeral.

He gazed from my stunned face to the open drawer, dark eyes full of thunder and lightning. "How dare you go through my personal things! Do I need to call security?"

I shook my head mutely.

He frowned, hands on hips. "I don't want to see you in

this office alone again." When I didn't respond, he whispered with finality, "Go on! Get out of my sight!"

I slunk to the floor, grabbed my pack, and oozed out the door, the lowest slime on the face of the earth.

"Violet!" Mr. Soloman hurried down the hall, recognizing me despite my ectoplasmic state. "Sorry I'm late. Musical classrooms. Let's see if Room 206 is free."

My life—from tragedy to comedy, like the Janus masks. Was there nothing in between?

★　★　★

There was. Mr. Soloman showed me a videotape of some very unfunny original comedy, several losing routines from a few years back.

"The performers shall remain nameless," he announced with tact, settling into the student desk next to me. "I just want you to learn from their mistakes. Now, forget about the delivery and concentrate on how the sketches are written."

Onscreen, a tall boy in a suit and tie droned on about a marine expedition to find the elusive "sea ostrich." I giggled once, when he first gave an odd rooster-sounding call to summon the bird, but by the fifteenth bellow I felt nauseated.

"Pretty awful, huh?" said Mr. Soloman, nodding. He stopped the tape with the remote. "What's wrong with this picture?"

We both agreed that the repetitive crowing overshadowed anything that might have been funny about the piece.

"Which parts do you think *could* have been funny?" he pressed.

"Well, maybe if he had used the characters' own words,

instead of just narrating, telling us blah blah blah, here's how we caught the sea ostrich. Who cares?"

Mr. Soloman threw me a grin and said, "Exactly! You have just asked the fundamental question of all great writing: Who cares?" He plugged in another video. "That is your job–to make the audience care. Once they care, you've got them in the palm of your hand. You can make them laugh, cry, or wet themselves."

"Or all three at once?"

"If you so choose."

"So how do I make them care?"

He nodded at the monitor.

Another boy in a suit and tie began his routine from his seat. When the coach said "Begin," he hesitated a moment, then jumped up from his chair with a loud baby cry and ran to the stage like someone was chasing him.

Once at his mark, he looked both ways and sighed with relief. "If you have a brother or sister–or just know someone who does–be on the lookout." Again, he checked both ways. "Be on the lookout for Superbaby: faster than a speeding tricycle . . . stronger than the family dog . . . able to leap tall playpens in a single bound . . . it's Superbaby!"

The routine had both Mr. Soloman and me cracking up by the end. Superbaby did terrible things to bedrooms, computers, Walkmans. Mark was eleven and still like that. I could totally relate.

"Got you right here"–Mr. Soloman mimed a punch to his gut–"didn't it?"

I nodded.

"Why?"

I shrugged.

"Two words." Mr. Soloman squinted and leaned over conspiratorially. "Universal humor," he said, settling back. "Everybody has experienced a willful baby—or knows someone who has. *That's* what you're going for. That common denominator."

I particularly liked this boy's style. "What about that entrance, screaming and running?" I said.

"Never mind that for now," my coach said. "You have an instinct for performing or you wouldn't be here. That will take care of itself. In O.C., writing comes first, theater comes second."

He got up and began putting videos in boxes. "I'm giving you until next Tuesday to come up with a draft. It doesn't have to be complete, but at least get a concept on paper."

"Like what kind of concept?"

He wagged a finger at me. "*Original* comedy. Not your speech coach's idea of a joke."

I pouted.

"Ah, ah, chin up. Give it a try. You'll be surprised what you come up with."

"That's what I'm afraid of," I said, sticking the information sheets he'd given me into my folder.

"Fear can be funny," Mr. Soloman insisted. "Make me laugh."

"I'll try."

"If you don't, I'll just get the hook."

Or The Ax, I thought. He'd probably be glad to get rid of me. "Okay, okay. See you next Tuesday, Mr. Soloman."

12

I figured I'd spend the rest of the school week waiting for ideas to hit, then write the speech on the weekend. The fact sheet said I had to fill eight minutes, tops. No "inappropriate" subject matter. No swearing.

It would never make an HBO special, but I was sure I could come up with something better than that sea ostrich sketch. I kept my ears peeled for comedy all week. On Wednesday, my piano teacher's dog started howling during my lesson, which was funny, just not funny enough to laugh about for eight minutes.

Thursday, I dropped by the Rise & Walk to see Mom after school. Somebody had donated six naked mannequins for the tax write-off, and Mom had to dress them before she could sell them; it *was* a church basement, after all, and naked doesn't belong in church. Unfortunately, naked was probably "inappropriate" for speech team too, or that would've been a hoot. I was laughing so hard by the time Mom put together an ensemble for Mannequin Number Three (ski parka, fishnet stockings, wing tips, and sombrero) that I had to go home.

Nothing was funny about Friday. From the moment I woke up, Abuela and Abuelo loaded me down with chores, preparations for the big domino party that would start at sundown. They ran the games on island time.

"*Ay*, Violeta, *por favor* load the dish*eh*washer for me," Abuela begged as I was trying to get out the door to the bus. She had been up long before Mark and me, starting a batch of *congrís* and stirring up pastry for the homemade éclairs. I couldn't complain when the eats were this good.

That afternoon, I helped Abuelo find an extension cord and move the stereo out to the porch. He pawed excitedly through a large CD case that he'd brought with him from Miami. "*Mira*, Violeta, *Fifty Years of Tito Puente*. This one is my favorite. *¿Cómo se dice* disc jockey *en inglés?*"

"In English? It's *disc jockey*, Abuelo."

"Ah, the same. ¡*Yo soy el rey de los* Disc Jockeys!"

I kissed the top of his bald head. "You are king of the *disc jockeys*, Abuelo." My Spanish was really improving, thanks to those cognates.

★ ★ ★

The guests started to arrive as salmony-colored clouds arched toward sunset, netting the sky. Mom and I were standing door duty.

84

"*¡Hola!* Diane. *¿Qué pasa?*"

"Welcome, it's been ages!" They volleyed hugs and kisses, shot them my way.

"*¡Qué linda!* Violet. How you've grown!" Lies, but good ones.

"Where is Lupita? *Y* Teodoro?"

Abuela was manning the kitchen, Abuelo was asleep. Yes, asleep. Guests would come and go all weekend, and somebody had to take the late hosting shift.

We sent everyone past the buffet in the living room, where many lingered, and on out to the porch, where Dad was holding court in his domino kingdom. You could hear "The Sky Is Crying" or "Baby Please Don't Go" blasting from the porch and Chucho barking up a fuss from behind my bedroom door, where he'd been safely stashed. The house smelled of garlicky *frijoles negros* and frying *plátanos*–green plantain chips, the kind I liked; they'd be salty-sweet and too hot to eat, but in no time they would disappear, leaving just an oil-spotted paper towel and spilled salt on the plate.

The little kids who'd come ran through the house like their hair was on fire, and my brother, Mark, suddenly five years old again, ran after them. It was beyond me how Abuelo could nap. I cruised through the living room and over to the designated drivers' table for one of Abuelo's nonalcoholic concoctions, Piña No-Nada, a piña colada whose secret ingredient was a shot of cold *café.* If I started drinking these now, I'd be wide awake for driver's ed by summer school.

I hung a left at the hallway and proceeded toward the

players' porch. Thankfully, the smoking section—two card tables sporting ashtrays and beer mugs full of Corona y Coronas—had been moved outside.

"*¡Hola!* Violeta." A grown cousin, Marianao, grabbed me in a hug, exhaling cigar smoke in my ear. Apparently she hadn't read the NO FUMAR signs. Marianao wore a skintight pink and green floral print dress, low in the neck and high in the skirt, and her dark hair was pinned up in an elaborate 'do. The cigar added a bizarre twist to her costume, but at least it was in character.

"Marianao, long time no see," I said, squeezing back. I smoothly guided her out the screen door into the tiki-torched yard, where she squealed at another long-lost somebody. Like I said, we hadn't seen much of these folks from the old neighborhood since Abuela and Abuelo flew south. They were an exotic foreign species to me.

Mark, in his ball cap and shorts as usual, ran around the corner of the house, followed by a chain of yelling kids dressed in Sunday clothes. "Vi, Mom says come to the kitchen right now!" he called over the noise, and kept on going. They zigzagged between tables, guests, and tiki torches, miraculously hitting none of them, and disappeared around the other side of the house.

★ ★ ★

The whole weekend was like that, like stepping onto a carousel ride gone berserk. Friday night, I fell asleep to the alternate clacking of dominoes and Tito Puente's *timbales*. The only time I could get a dime in edgewise on one of the packed porch tables was when I woke up in the middle of the night to use the bathroom and found Abuelo and two friends still playing. The stereo had been switched low, and an empty, grease-dotted *plátanos* plate sat on the floor beside them. I picked it up and ran a wet finger around it, finishing off the last of the salt.

The men signaled me to throw in a dime, and a new game began.

"This is the life, *eh,* Teo?" asked one of Abuelo's friends. "This remind me of *las fiestas navideñas* back in Cuba."

Abuelo nodded. He wore his party shirt, a pastel pink, yellow, and blue striped *guayabera,* over his usual dark trousers. "*Sí, claro que sí.* Padrino use to hang *las hamacas* in the *eh*stables, *para las siestas.*"

"Like a sleepover, Abuelo?"

He grinned an ocean of teeth at me in my baby-doll pajamas and sweater. "*Sí, como un* Sleep Over. People would come and go for many days, and Padrino would roast the *lechón* in the big pit, and there were cards and dominoes, never stopping."

The four of us at the table sighed.

"Those were the days," Abuelo said.

★　★　★

Chucho needed a run on Saturday morning after being penned up in my room most of the night before. The hot spell had left town overnight; outside, in my shorts and gym T-shirt, I felt that crisp September bite that said, "*Adiós,* summer!"

Chucho felt it too. He skittered down the blacktop toward the street like a pup, until we reached the spot on the sidewalk in front of the Vespuccis' house where old Mrs. Vespucci tossed stale bread for the birds. Sparrows and robins squawked in all directions as Chucho found an almost-whole kaiser roll and chunked it down in one lump, like a python.

I scooped him up in my arms before Mrs. V. could spot us through the oversized slats of her skeletal venetian blinds and yell through the screen door. *"Cabrito,"* I scolded Chucho, releasing him a few paces later and jogging off down Woodtree.

We got back and went to the kitchen for a drink, where I found Mom in high gear; today was Abuela's day to play. Ovals of kielbasa sausage were lined up on the counter, at the ready. Mom checked on some steaming cabbage, stirred a tomato sauce, and drained a pan of browned ground beef, practically at once. I licked my finger and stuck it in a plate of powdered sugar left over from making kolachke cookies. This was better than Christmas. Maybe I'd get a chance to win some simoleons today too.

"Mom, can I have a few bucks for dimes?"

She threw me a harried look from a sinkful of suds and dirty pots. "How about an even exchange?"

"But I just walked the dog!" I sighed. "Oh, all right." I washed a few pans, and Mom let me lick the brownie bowl and told me to take some singles from her purse.

"Thanks, Mom!"

I put Chucho outside on his tether and hunted down my brother. He sat in the garage surrounded by patio furniture, sorting through a huge box of old golf balls he'd found.

"Mark! I need you to watch Chucho today. Make sure none of the little kids lets him off the leash."

He dropped a fluorescent yellow ball into a bucket of soapy water as if I weren't there.

"Okay?" I prompted.

Mark set aside two balls with gashes in them and dropped a scuffed Titleist in the water bucket, saying nothing.

"Okay?" I said again, giving his Cubs hat brim a tweak.

"Hey!" he yelped. "Why can't you watch out for Chucho? I'm busy."

"I just took him for a walk, he's not my responsibility."

He bared his gums at me. "Oh yes he is too. You're the one having the keent-sy party. You're the one who has to be responsible."

I opened my mouth to deny it, and my brother jumped up and ran away, leaving his golf balls soaking.

What a baby. I stamped my foot and had turned to leave when a box on a shelf over the washer and dryer caught my eye: RIT. It was a box of red dye Mom had used to make a Santa suit out of a pair of pajamas several years ago. Could dye go bad?

I took out a handful of tabs and dropped them in Mark's golf ball water. Then I went out to the playing porch to look for some trouble.

★   ★   ★

In between siestas that afternoon, I lost my shirt to my grandmother. No matter the configuration of players at the table, Abuela and I battled neck and neck, and she rallied to win at the last minute. I was beginning to think she carried around a double-blank tile in the pocket of her silver gaucho skirt or its matching jacket.

"*Lo siento,* Violeta, *pero* I win again!" she sang cheerfully from pimiento-colored lips, reaching for the pot as the other players commiserated with me, one game after another. Still, I kept coming back for more.

After my dinner break, I had to cadge some more dimes off Dad, who was running the change exchange. He wore one of those canvas coin pouches the volunteers used at the Lincolnville Petunia Festival every year. Blue plaid pants and penny loafers stuck out below the pouch, and above, he'd tucked in his favorite sunshine-yellow long-sleeved shirt with the monkeys on it. Dad roamed the porch, in his element: A guest would hand him a five, and he'd count out fifty dimes like he was filling a prescription. You knew he'd never make a mistake.

Unfortunately, he knew exactly how many doses he'd already given me. "That's it for tonight, *chiquitica,*" he said sternly, doling out five measly coins. "Your friend is here, by the way."

"Leda?"

He nodded toward the backyard.

She'd made it. "Hey, Leed!" I called, finding her at one of the smoking tables outside.

She waved for quiet. "*Shhh,* Paz. I'm concentrating."

Leda, my cousin Marianao, and a heavyset man with a shirt just like Abuelo's all bent over a long domino chain, each player with two pieces left to go.

Marianao had returned tonight, this time dressed in a white cotton halter dress with a slit skirt. Her blood-red lacquered nails fingered the two dominoes rhythmically. She and the other man had parked a couple of steaming

Coronas in the ashtray, one of them smeared with red lipstick. Leda, in a T-shirt that said LOVE YOUR MOTHER over a photo of planet Earth, eyed the board shrewdly. She feinted with one piece, then went to the other, laying it quietly on the end of the chain.

"Caramba," growled Marianao, knocking.

The man laid down a low number.

"Caramba," said Leda, in a damn good accent. She knocked.

"Se acabó," grumbled Marianao, knocking.

But the man couldn't play either, and they all ended up adding up their points. Leda won by two.

Marianao reached for the mug on the table and handed Leda a cigar.

13

As Sunday dawned, I padded out to the porch in bare feet and pajamas, hoping to find a few forgotten dimes stuck in the edges of a domino board or under some chair cushions. I came across Abuelo asleep on the old couch, party shirt crumpled, snores escaping his lips like blasts of percussion. He was probably dreaming of the hammocks at Padrino's farm in Cuba. I didn't have the heart to wake him. And I refrained from going through his pockets.

I got up early because today was C-Day: comedy day. The threat of a deadline might help; hadn't Mr. Soloman said that fear could be funny? I decided that something funny was going to happen today if it killed me.

I went around front to get the newspaper and discovered I wasn't the first one up. Mark squatted in the driveway, hosing off a pile of pink golf balls. When I turned to retreat, he spied me.

"You!" He turned the hose on me, but the stream wouldn't reach.

I stuck my fingers in my mouth, crossed my eyes, and did a little dance. "What's wrong with your shirt, little brother?" I needled him, noticing the pink splotches and handprints on his white T-shirt.

He picked up a handful of wet golf balls and threw them at me, and I fled.

Abuela entered the kitchen while I was mixing up some frozen orange juice. She looked tired and had neglected to style her hair or iron her bathrobe before breakfast for a change. Her silver hair, creased from sleep, hung down to the middle of her back.

"Sit down, Abuela," I said, handing her a glass of juice. "I'll make you some *café*." I found the ancient stovetop espresso maker in the drainer and the Café Bustelo in the fridge. I measured the coffee and water and set the pot on the stove to boil.

"All that winning really takes it out of you, doesn't it, Abuela?" I teased.

She flashed me a grin untouched by lipstick this morning. "The ween-ing, it is good," she said. "I stay up till two-thirty *anoche*." She closed her eyes and took a long swallow of orange juice. "Ahh!" she sighed.

We divided up the newspaper and read in silence for a while. Then the coffeemaker started to burp, and I pulled a demitasse and my poodle mug from the cupboard and poured us each a cup. I loaded mine down with milk and sugar and began sipping while Abuela performed her ritual: a single shot of *café,* two heaping teaspoons of sugar, and a pinch of salt for good luck—then down the hatch.

"Ahh!" she sighed again.

I figured her throat must look like the inside of a volcano, but it seemed to work for her.

"I'm glad you're having a good time, Abuela," I said. "You know, Abuelo was saying this reminds him of the domino parties in Cuba on his godfather's farm."

She puckered her lips together and nodded slowly. "For us, was the club." The light came into her eyes again as she thought back. "We use to love to play domino at El Habano. I was known as a very good player."

"El Habano? That's the place with the chandeliers and marble columns and stuff?"

She nodded. "*Sí.* Is where I make my *quince.*"

"Your *quince?*"

Wow. I'd been that close to the information before? Abuela guarded her secrets like gold. I shook my head in aggravation and pressed my luck. "In a pink dress, Abuela?" I wanted to hear her say it.

A brief smile crossed her lips. "In the pink dress," she let herself recall. "*Por supuesto,* such a dress! And such a day. Was *una fiesta grande,* with the court of twenty-eight, and *flores* everywhere . . . And Papi . . . *ay,* so handsome in his white suit."

"And what about you?"

"Me? I am *como una princesa* in a fairy book." She

paused. "But is no the dress and the flowers or the friends watching that are important to me."

"No?"

I'd thought they were the point.

"*Sí,*" Abuela said, the faraway light still glowing softly in her eyes. "Not those things. Was the *momento* after the waltz, when Papi and I make *el paseo* together. He says to me, 'Guadalupe Inez, *m'ija,* I am always here for you. If ever you have hard times, remember today and know that your *papá* is here to give you strength.'" She shook her head, her long hair falling about her shoulders. "I never forget this."

"And your dad . . ."

"He die in Coo-ba. Is a long time ago. But always he is with me." She flashed a true grin. "Was a great domino player, Papi. *¡El mejor!* I think I inherit some-sing from him."

I smiled. "I know you did!"

She sighed low and long.

After a pause, she said, "Violeta, *óyeme.* I have *una idea* for today. Is a beeg day, many people."

Abuelo was to re-create Padrino's pig roast, only on a smaller scale involving a marinated fresh ham and the Weber. Everyone my grandparents knew from the city would show up for that.

"My *idea* is this: to put a table for to sign up the *eh*sponsors for your *quince* party. We can put right by the front door, *¿no?* You can sit there *con un* sign: 'Violeta Paz, *La Quinceañera.*'"

I put my mug down. "Trying to get me off the domino tables, Abuela? Very sneaky."

She gave me a light *cocotazo*—a domino knock to the noggin. *"¡Ay, Dios, esta muchacha . . . !"* Then she grinned again. I liked her lips this color. "So, how do you think?"

Hmmm. A reception table might be just the vantage point I needed. I'd see everyone who came in or went out, and I could plumb them for humor. It just might be worth a giggle. "Not bad, Abuela. Should I wear my dress?"

"¡Ay, no, chica!"

"Just kidding, just kidding. A sign's a good idea, though. I'll go make one after breakfast."

Abuela smiled, and the wrinkles seemed to fall from her robe and under her eyes at the same time. *"Gracias pa' el café,"* she said.

★　★　★

All our card tables were in use, but Mom's African-violet table had wheels and was just about the right height. I made my sign and went downstairs to get the plant stand. Mom's seven pots of African violets greeted me from the tiled floor beneath the purple-blue grow light—and the table was gone. But a telltale trail of tiny pink droplets led back up the steps.

Further investigation drew me out the front door to the open garage, where I found the plant stand parked, a tackle box full of dimes open on top, and my brother in his Cubs hat behind it. At his feet sat a bushel basket of golf balls and a pile of plastic kitchen bags. Propped against the table, a huge poster in Mark's handwriting announced: SALE—GOLF BALLS, 1 BUCK.

"God, Vi," Mark said, scowling, "d'you know how long it took me to get these clean? I could've killed you."

"You're *selling* these?"

"Sure, I've made six bucks already."

It wasn't even ten o'clock on a Sunday morning. Yet here came another group of customers, stopping their cars by the refrigerator-box sign in our driveway: QUALITY USED GOLF BALLS. I grimaced and went back into the house.

A little later Mom gave me an old tin TV tray with a faded picture of a deer on it and told me to set it up out back, and take Chucho with me. He was eating the frills off the party toothpicks.

I chose a spot under the maple tree, midway between the domino tables and the barbecue grill, and staked Chucho next to me. He went into a little snit fit in the grass, rolling and snuffling; then he stretched, yawned, and gave a little squeak at the end. I scratched him under his pointy chin. "I have got to do some math homework, boy," I told him, pulling out a notebook, and he immediately curled up at my feet and went to sleep. My sentiments exactly.

The hard-core players, Marianao included, began to arrive around noon, and more guests trickled in throughout the day. The baby-blue sky and Abuelo's coals burning down in the grill lured most people out back for a while. Many of them carried old bread bags full of golf balls. But my TV-tray business was booming too. As was Dad's *Best of Buddy Guy* on the stereo.

Buddy tweaked his guitar hard in the background as a cousin a few years older than me approached my *quince* stand.

"Eva, long time no see!" At least I remembered her name. Eva had come straight from Mass at St. Ignacio's. She wore a navy blue tie-back dress, stockings, heels, and pearl earrings and carried a clutch purse. She wrote her family down for the party flowers.

"*Muchas gracias,* Eva. That's awful generous."

"I didn't make my *quince* when I was fifteen," she said ruefully. "My sister Cristina's wedding broke the bank that year. I think Mami and Papi are feeling guilty."

"Guilty's as good as generous," I said.

She leaned over to exchange air kisses before saying good-bye.

★ ★ ★

The blues on the stereo switched to salsa, and Abuelo brought the pork roast out to the grill. The yard had filled with relatives and friends, and, I suspected, a few of Mark's customers who'd hung around for a freebie. Cigar plumes from the domino tables mingled with briquette smoke, forming a mushroom cloud that drifted slowly toward the Vespucci yard. A gang of little kids played a dangerous, high-speed game of horseshoes on one corner of the lawn, all shrieking at once. Someone turned up the music.

I jogged around the house, past Mark wrestling a golf ball from a stubborn cousin, and through the front door. Harsh laughter rattled from the kitchen. I walked in to find one of Dad's relatives wearing the toaster cozy on his head and singing into a spatula in a booming voice, in Spanish.

"*HA!*" yelled my mother, followed by three imaginary beats. She dropped her garlic press on the counter and fell into line behind him. Abuela's sister, Tía Sara, took a swig from a pitcher she was stirring and grabbed Mom by the hips, chanting, "Cha-cha-*cha,* cha-cha-*cha.*"

I might have missed the punch line, but this looked like fun! I latched on behind Mom, and we snaked out of the kitchen and past the buffet, picking up Dad's friend Rudi, Eva's mom and dad, and a bewildered-looking stranger carrying a bag of golf balls, and we all congaed down the hallway to the back porch.

Our cries were swallowed by trumpets and drumbeats and a singer's voice; then we pushed through the porch and out to the backyard. Marianao shimmied over in a tight black minidress. "Cha-cha-*cha,* cha-cha-*cha!*" repeated Tía Sara as more joined the line.

Abuelo, manning the Weber, saw us coming and started clacking his barbecue tongs like castanets. Unable to resist, he tossed his squirt bottle to an innocent by-stander and joined the dance.

"Cha-cha-*cha,* cha-cha-*cha!*" we cried, chugging around the house. I motioned to Mark out front, but he crossed his arms and pointed to his inventory. Dad's cousin at the head of the line spun into a tight spiral, which made everybody dizzy, then whipped us back out into a straight line and around the corner of the house. A siren down the street mingled with blazing conga drums from the stereo as we returned to the backyard, to the sight of—flames on the grill.

The roast was on fire.

I've never seen Abuelo move so fast. He catapulted past the horseshoe players, grabbed a two-pronged fork from the grill, and speared the roast in one motion. The marinade on the meat burned merrily as Abuelo hopped in a circle, swear-ing in Spanish and trying not to trip over Chucho's taut leash. Inside, someone cranked the music even louder.

Chucho began to howl. One of the little kids yelled "Fire! Fire!" until the rest took it up. Some of the grown-ups chimed in, half of them howling, as Abuelo whipped the flaming meat into a bonfire by dancing madly through the backyard. He ran for the metal tub of ice full of Old Style and Cokes. Then, looking for all the world like the Cuban Statue of Liberty, he raised the burning roast high, swearing, and with a great hissing and steaming, he doused the thing in the ice.

At this particular moment, around the corner of the house strolled two uninvited visitors in blue suits and shiny shoes: Lincolnville's finest.

The cops.

The grim-faced man and woman surveyed the scene, taking in the blaring music, howling dog, reeling guests, and gambling tables—not to mention the smoking, burnt lump in the beer cooler and my grandfather, dripping, beside it—and shook their heads.

Abuelo straightened up, smoothed his soot-smudged party shirt.

Somebody killed the stereo.

Abuelo cleared his throat and said hoarsely, "Officers, I can 'splain. I can 'splain everything."

★ ★ ★

An hour later, my family and I sat in somber silence at the fake-marble kitchen table over two bags of White Castles and the leftover fruit punch. The cops had broken up the party, sending everyone home with a warning, and told Mark he couldn't sell golf balls anymore without a peddler's license. Abuela and Abuelo appeared suitably chastised over the ruckus; Mark, hunched over in the Death Throne, just pouted.

Although it was kind of embarrassing getting busted by the police (our neighbors had come out to watch the red and blue lights twirl around and see Mark pack up his golf ball stand), all in all I thought it had been a successful way to end a party. Everybody went home wanting more, there was a ton of leftovers, and I had just witnessed the most bizarre spectacle of my fifteen years on Earth.

And so I found my Original Comedy material.

14

I plunged into my script. I mean, you can't make up stuff like Sunday's grand-slam ending to the domino party. And, as Abuelo had said good-naturedly afterward, if you can't laugh at yourself, who can you laugh at? All I had to do now was write down what happened . . . and then get up in front of a bunch of strangers and act it out, over and over again.

The horror.

Speech team was supposed to prep me for my big entrance into the world of women in front of God and my long-lost relatives. But what kind of logic was this: Getting up onstage in front of a strange audience supposedly makes getting up onstage in front of a strange audience less terrifying. That's like saying that sticking your hand in a blender will make it so much easier the next time around.

Still, I wasn't about to quit. Like those Janus masks, I'd always had a love/hate relationship with performing. That first step is a doozy. But once you make it over the fear hump, it's smooth sailing.

Mr. Soloman had said a good way to get started was to come up with three points that tied together, building a beginning, middle, and end.

That was easy; I started with Mark's golf balls, moved on to Marianao's domino game, and finished with Abuelo's *pièce de résistance,* the blackened roast. Then I read it out loud to see how long it was.

By dinnertime, I had it up to five minutes. Still short, but good enough for a first draft. The premise was that the cops show up at Abuelo's party and throw me in jail with my family, a fate worse than death. I'd lay it on Mr. Soloman on Tuesday.

★　★　★

Monday afternoon, with the weather just right for September, Janell, Leda, and I sat in different corners of Janell's bedroom, reading. Sometimes we did that, hung out in the same room, not talking, just reading; together, but not together. I'd gone deep into Le Guin's Earthsea, myself; Janell was off playing Chicago P.I. with V. I. Warshawski, and who knew what trip Leda was on. She had burrowed into the beanbag chair over by the stairs, while Janell lay stretched out on the amazingly thick alpaca rug by her bed and I took the window seat.

I loved sitting in a window seat, loved holding a book on my lap there; it felt so Jane Eyre. The bay window and adjacent French doors let in golden-brown afternoon light, dappled by a birch's mellowing leaves. A fresh-cut grass scent seeped into the room behind the clicking of the push mower as Janell's mom worked outside in the yard.

Janell's bedroom ran the whole width of the back of her house and opened out onto the deck. When her dad and mom divorced, Janell and her mother converted their den into the most fabulous bedroom in the world. They'd designed different zones for sleeping, studying, and dance workouts, each painted a different tasteful color—eggplant, mustard, kale green.

Tasteful, in fact, sums up Janell Kelly, and her mother, Alicia Pennpierson, a slender, dark-haired woman with an alluring cat purr of a Southern accent. I've known both of them most of my life. Alike enough to be mistaken for sisters, my friend and her mom are my idols. But I'd never tell them that.

It was hard to switch from saying "Mrs. Kelly" to "Ms. Pennpierson" after the divorce, but easier than trying to talk to Janell about any of it. That happened in seventh grade, and Janell is just now beginning to mention her dad and stuff. Other than that, she always seems more together, more sophisticated and focused, than always-at-loose-ends Violet Paz. I guess that's why we get along so well.

The other tough switch came after I met Leda, whose appeal, I admit, has to grow on some people. Luckily, Janell let it grow, not like a well-tended rosebush, granted—Janell at first merely tolerated Leda—but more like a moss.

Gradually, though, the two arose from the swamp of their indifference. And now we were three.

"Aau-he-hem." Leda cleared her throat and thrashed on the beanbag chair for a new position. "Kelly. Paz. Will you listen to this?"

Janell and I looked up from our reading and mentally high-fived each other from across the room. Leda is usually the one to break the silence.

"Guys, I have got to go to Paris immediately!" She stabbed a finger at her open book.

"I thought you planned to go with Willie after graduation," I said.

"I broke up with that idiot. He showed up at the last PETA meeting in a leather jacket. No, no, I'm going to Paris on my own, as soon as possible. Did you know you can take dogs into bistros there?"

"But you don't have a dog," Janell pointed out.

Leda's eyes burned blue intensity. "I know, but it's the *idea* of it—dogs in a restaurant? That just goes to show how cool the French are."

I thought of Chucho being left to graze happily on the floor at White Castle. "And," I said, laughing, "you'd appreciate your food a whole lot more."

"Or at least be more protective of it," said Janell, smiling.

Leda, still serious, went on. "Then there's the whole eat-or-be-eaten aspect. You know, little Fifi looking on as *le maestro* gloms down a rack of lamb."

"There but for the grace of God go I." Janell nodded.

"HA!" I borrowed Mom's laugh. "By the way, Leed, you're mixing your French and Spanish again."

The reading mood was broken.

"Let's go get something to eat," Janell said.

★   ★   ★

Janell's virginal refrigerator in the chaste white kitchen always holds a huge bowl of fruit salad and little more, unless her mom is cooking one of her fabulous fried-chicken dinners. We made waffle cones of frozen yogurt with the fruit on top.

Leda took a bite first and pursed her lips. "Fruit tastes weird with—what flavor is this?"

Janell picked up the frozen yogurt container. "It says vanilla, but . . ." Hesitantly, she peeled back the lid. "Uh-oh."

We looked at her.

"You'd better not eat any more of that," she told Leda.

I examined my softening cone. The yogurt had black specks in it, but sometimes real vanilla looks like that.

Leda froze her jaw, trying not to swallow. "Well, what is it?" she demanded through the food.

Janell twisted a foot behind her. "Um, it's bacon grease," she mumbled. "Mom uses it for frying—keeps it in the freezer . . ."

Leda's eyes said it all.

She bolted from the white dinette to the sink, bent, and let it fly. A lot more than the bite of ice cream was recycled.

Janell and I just stood there, cones melting. Then we simultaneously got grossed out and threw them in the white enameled sink. Janell turned on the garbage disposal. Ever the tactful one, I started to belly laugh. Normally-in-check Janell watched Leda hanging over the sink and busted out too.

Upon which Leda gasped a breath and shouted, "Get me a glass of water!"

Janell, laughing now in mime and resembling my mother in one of her aftershocks, found a glass in one of the white windowed cabinets and got Leda some water from the tap. Leda gulped and spit, gulped and spit, till the water was gone. Then she just kept spitting into the sink.

"I . . . can't . . . believe . . . you!" she said in bursts between spits.

"I'm sorry, Leed," Janell tried.

Her smile was met by a drooly look of disbelief from our friend. "I'm a vegetarian, Kelly!"

Janell forced her lips into a straight line. "It's terrible for you, I know," she said. "But it was an accident."

"I don't 'accidentally' eat meat!"

"Fat," I corrected.

"Meat! Fat! I don't care! How could you do this to me?" She cast eyes on Janell, blinking a furious SOS.

"It *was* an accident. . . . ," I said, as surprised as Janell at Leda's wrath.

Leda spit into the sink once more. "Well, it won't happen again. I can't even be around you two!" She wiped her mouth on her shirtsleeve and stomped out the front door.

One *dama* down, I thought, one to go.

15

Janell and I were surprised to see Leda wave us over in Room C206 the next afternoon at our speech team meeting. We exchanged wary glances but went and sat next to her.

"Hey, dudes, what's up? Ready to face our impending speech tournament doom?"

I hesitated. "What about yesterday?"

"Yeah, about never wanting to see us again?" Janell added.

Leda shrugged. "Oh, that. I channeled it. I can't help it if you guys are pathetic."

I sighed, knowing that no matter what she said, she'd never forgive us for that one.

She pulled out her ratty purple notebook covered with stick-figure doodles and opened it. "See? I channeled the bad energy into my Oratory routine. 'Plows, Not Cows,' I call it. I went home and wrote the whole thing in about half an hour. I showed it to The Ax at lunch today, and he loved it."

"Then I guess you should thank us," Janell said dryly.

We hadn't finalized our routines yet. "Mine's not done," I said to Leda. "Maybe you should piss *me* off."

Janell slapped me a wry five.

I looked around but didn't see Clarence Williams anywhere. Ms. Joyner, resplendent in a flowing batik robe, manhandled the crowd into submission as usual and got started. We were prepping for our first tournament, the following Saturday at Taylor Park.

Ms. Joyner described the timetable: two preliminary rounds, plus a final, then the awards ceremony. "You should have all received the rules for your events from your coaches, so you already know that you have to be on time for your rounds, or the team loses points with your disqualification. Even though these are individual events, a team trophy is at stake too. Please make it a habit to wear a watch. You have a little over a week to prepare." She looked up at the booth. "Are you ready, Rick?"

"Ten-four." The Ax's voice cut through the sound system like piano wire. "Let's see what kind of blood we've got this year."

Ms. Joyner called everybody center stage one by one, according to event. Janell sailed away first, along with another sharply dressed girl named Cherise, to represent Verse Reading. I saw Gina from my gym class with the Dramatic Interpretation group, which included Zeno Clark and his duet partner, Trish Lazlo, the favorites. Competitors in Humorous Interpretation, Oratorical Declamation, Radio Speaking, and Prose Reading filed down to the stage. When Extemporaneous Speaking was called, Clarence still hadn't shown up.

Leda was the lone Original Oratory candidate, and I shared Original Comedy with Vera Campbell, a junior who sometimes sold the school newspaper; the rest of the team members I'd either met at the first meeting or never seen before in my life. It's a big school.

"Okay, gang," Ms. Joyner said, surveying us all. "We're a team now. You can sit down."

As we filtered back to our seats, she delivered final instructions. "Clean, neat clothing is a must! Do not talk during your round. Do not ask the judges for your ranks; you'll get critique sheets later. Do not ask the judges how you did," she said with a smile. "You'll do fine."

"And above all," the tech mike boomed, its operator sounding not unlike the great and powerful Oz, *"no* yelling during the awards ceremony. Whether we win, or whether we lose."

A few wails rose. The guy in front of me argued, "But everyone at Brighton South went *nuts* at State last year!"

"Those are the Tri-Dist rules," Mr. Axelrod hushed into the microphone, as though issuing a prayer.

"And we have a reputation to uphold," Ms. Joyner added, nodding. Tri-Dist had won State a few years before. "So be on the bus at seven-forty-five next Saturday, bring a lunch, and be ready to compete." She shrugged at the booth. "Rick?"

"Just one more thing, ladies and gentlemen: Practice like crazy. And kick ass!"

★　★　★

Mr. Soloman liked my ideas for the speech; he told me to add a few minutes to it before our meeting the next Tuesday. So I headed for the source of my material. I went home.

For a going-away dinner that night, Abuela made *arroz con pollo,* everyone's favorite dish except Mark's. At least there was *flan* for dessert. As I sat down next to my brother at the kitchen table, I saw the look on his face, a sort of Cro-Magnon glare that spelled "foul mood." It had been his unhappy fate to take the last turn in the Death Throne, and he faced a steaming plate of chicken and yellow rice, which he hated. On top of that, the sorry Cubs had just slipped out of play-off contention. I was devastated myself. Mark wasn't even wearing his hat.

"So that's what color your hair is," I said.

He ignored me and kept picking the little canned peas out of his rice. He had already made a pile of pimientos on one side of his plate.

Abuelo stirred in his soft chair and sighed. "*Bueno,* another year down the drain for *los* Cubs, no? I am happy to go home to my Marlins. They are going to win the World Series this year."

Mark cut him a look and pushed some food around on his plate.

Dad thought to salve Mark's wound with the old standby Cub-fan reply: "Well, Mark, there's always next season, *eh?*"

Mark nodded numbly and rocked in his seat, trying to get some blood to flow to his butt.

We attacked our plates with varying degrees of gusto, and Abuela said it was time to talk about the guest list for my party.

"How about *my* party?" asked Mark.

"Your birthday isn't until January," Mom said.

"Sho?" Mark raged through a mouthful of chewed-up rice. He choked it down. "Her party's not till May! Why is it always Violet, Violet, Violet?"

"Because you're not mature enough to make your *quince*," I said.

"Claro que sí," murmured Abuela.

While Mark sulked, we turned to the matter at hand. My sponsors had been mostly lined up and a budget set. We had decided on eighty guests, a number that seemed too few to fill a hall and too many to perform for.

"Can we invite Mrs. Lowenstein?" I asked, meaning my piano teacher. I've known her since I was four.

"I think we should invite the Caprizios," Mom said, stabbing a fork with two peas stuck to it at Dad. "They asked us to that New Year's party last year."

"Wait a minute," I said, "I don't even know the Caprizios. And kids weren't invited to that party."

*"Eh*stop it," Abuela cut in. "We *eh*start with the *familia*."

I counted on my fingers. "You, Abuelo, Mom, Dad, Tía Luci, Mark—"

Mark spoke up. "I'm not going."

Dad tilted his head and raised an eyebrow, as if considering the option himself.

"Forget it," I snapped with a steely look, and Dad shrugged. Mark made a fist with his lips.

"*Y* Juan Pedro *y* Arnalda," put in Abuelo.

"*Y* Sara *y* Roberto, *y los* Guerreros," said Abuela.

Mom and Dad joined the litany in Spanish.

With a primeval scowl, Mark muttered, "Who cares about some dumb Cuban party?"

Dad heard him. "What did you say, young man?"

"I said, this Cuba stuff sucks!" Mark pushed his numb behind up from the Throne.

Everybody stopped talking.

Fuming, and using the umpire's signal for player ejection, Dad ousted Mark from the room.

The Cubs loss *and* no dessert. I felt a pure sorrow for my brother at that moment and went out on a limb. "Dad, Mark shouldn't have to come to the party if he doesn't want to. You didn't go when you were growing up."

I could tell by Dad's expression that it was the showers for me too. Before he could give the sign, I got up from my chair and said, "I know, Ump, I know. I'm outta here." And, in solidarity, I left the field.

16

*E*ven if I had refrained from sticking up for Mark, it wouldn't have saved me from my impending appointment with Señora Flora, party planner to the stars. My dress had to go back to Chez Doll soon, and Señora Flora's sister was going to handle the dress replication, or whatever you'd call this guerrilla tailoring.

As Dad was putting the bags in the car for my grandparents' trip to the airport, Abuela handed me an envelope to give to Señora Flora. Mark and I had apologized the night before—in English—and Abuela had promised never again to make *arroz con pollo,* if that was what it did to Mark.

So Mark was happy.

But he wasn't on his way to see Señora Flora, a meeting I looked forward to with about as much enthusiasm as another class trip to Springfield, Illinois. I had visited the sixteenth president's hometown thousands of times during elementary school, but if forced to choose between hearing Lincoln's life story broadcast at his tomb once more or having Señora Flora size me up and dress me down, I'd be gathering brochures and buying log cabin figurines in a heartbeat.

I figured this Señora Flora for some fussy, ruffly type who harbored set ideas about how us *quince*-babes were supposed to look and act. She'd probably teach me the Cuban minuet. I wondered what was in Abuela's envelope, a fifty with the word *tradicional* scrawled across it?

Mom drove us to Arlington Heights and made me look for the street number when we got close. A compact blond brick building housed the salon, with the famed party planner's name up in Broadway-style lights: SEÑORA FLORA, FIESTERA DE LAS ESTRELLAS. Mom crowbarred us into a parking space, and I carried the dress box into the shop.

A tiny slip of a woman in a suit hunched over the front desk, reading a *Sun-Times* through the thickest glasses I had ever seen. She took in Mom's out-on-the-town ensemble—powder-blue knit skirt, red and white sailor blouse sewn all over with anchor buttons, plus her "sensible shoes," soot-colored nurse's oxfords bought at a uniform-store fire sale—and hoisted a magnified eyebrow. Apparently her glasses prescription was right on the money.

"*¿Nombre?*"

"We're Paz," said Mom.

This didn't impress the woman. *"¿Y quiénes se nos refieren?"*

"References?" Mom was taken aback. *"Mi suegra, Lupita Zarza."*

That was Abuela.

"¿Y hay otra . . . ?"

Now Mom was pissed. "Yeah, I've got another reference. The Pope! You want his number?"

This invented credential did impress the nearsighted woman. *"¡El Papa! Pues . . ."*

"We have an appointment with Señora Flora at four. Are you gonna get her?"

Our hostess jumped off her stool. *"Seguro, seguro, Doña Paz, cómo no, cómo no."* And she disappeared behind a blue curtain.

With a great rustling of fabric and clinking of metal bracelets, Señora Flora swished through the curtain, kissed Mom on two cheeks, and took the dress box out of my hands before you could say *cocotazo.*

"Buenas tardes, bienvenidas, welcome!" she said, taking a step back and getting a good look at me. I wore my rust-colored tunic outfit again, this time with a maroon T-shirt underneath and my favorite sandals.

Señora Flora gave me a nod and said, "You must be Violet. Lupita told me great things about you."

"Me too, you—too, that is," I said stupidly, even though Abuela had told me zip about her, except that her parties were so popular that she normally had a waiting list a mile long. But Abuela had an in.

How she knew Señora Flora, I couldn't imagine. The

party planner to the stars was, first of all, young; way younger than I'd expected. She must have been under forty, because she had good hands. I'd read in some magazine that you could always guess a woman's age by her hands, and it showed how hands look at different ages. The twenties and thirties hands hadn't looked too bad, but once those fingers hit forty, you could tell. Too many years, too many dishes.

Besides the smooth hands, Señora Flora had a shiny black pageboy with just a few gray hairs streaking it, chestnut eyes with big dark lashes, and a comfortable manner. She wore a long, sweeping silk dress in a bold abstract print that Ms. Joyner would have envied.

"Never mind my sister. Fauna gets carried away with security sometimes."

Fauna?

"She's very thorough," Mom said with a barb.

Señora Flora didn't seem to notice. "Step into my office. *Por favor,* this way."

★　★　★

Señora Flora was surprisingly businesslike. First off, we talked scale and we talked money. We filled in the blanks on her form: number of guests, type of refreshments, number in the court. Dressmaking and dance lesson fees. Invitations and party favors. Music and lights. Tux rentals and corsages. Mom obliged by showing her the plans in our "portfolio," a Snoopy notebook just like Mom's restaurant planner, with a twelve-month AT-A-GLANCE calendar stapled to the back cover.

When we had agreed on an affordable package, Señora

Flora sent Mom back to the waiting room. She said she wanted to talk to me alone.

I remembered Abuela's envelope and offered it to her, ready to defend myself against whatever pinkness it contained. "Señora Flora . . ."

"Call me Flora, *amiga.*"

"But isn't that your last name?"

She grinned sheepishly, tearing open the envelope. "It's Flora Markowicz. My mother is Cuban and my father was Polish. My parents' neighborhoods overlapped, and I'm the result."

"Me too—the opposite," I said, amazed. "Señora Markowicz?"

"You can drop the *Señora.* I'm not married. It just sounded like a catchy business name. Would you trust your once-in-a-lifetime party to a Señorita Markowicz?"

I had to admit, *Señora Flora's* had more of a ring to it.

Flora scanned Abuela's note—I didn't notice a money bribe in there—and folded it back into the envelope. Then she looked into my eyes with such unexpected feeling, I recoiled on the office couch we were sharing.

"What do you want from life, Violet?"

What kind of question was this? And what kind of answer did she want: the car-house-kids one; or the health–happiness–world peace one?

When in doubt, lie.

"Um, I want to become an emergency-room veterinarian and teach people about animals and stuff." This had been true several years back, before I realized that I was deathly allergic to cats and that I had no affinity for blood, two things that make a bad animal doctor.

"I mean personally. How do you see yourself?"

"Well . . ." I could either snow her now, or tell it to her straight. "Well, since you ask." I narrowed my eyes. "First of all, I'm not the *quince* type."

Her eyebrows flexed, but she said nothing.

"I don't wear dresses—haven't since grade school. A person has to choose their own style. Though I know Abuela doesn't think so. . . . And plus, I don't do slow dances, with or without my dad, and I don't know any of the Cuban customs." I thought that summed it up.

Flora nodded. "This is what you are not. How about what you are?"

"I am . . . someone who likes to watch sports but hates playing on teams. I've studied piano since I was four, but I don't know how to play the kind of music I really like. I'm on the speech team and I've done lots of skits and puppet shows, but I'm not really the onstage type of performer. It's like, I have a lot of half talents."

She nodded, still silent.

"I guess I want them to be full talents, and that's the kind of person I want to be."

"Anything else? Any other hopes, dreams, aspirations?"

I considered. "I wish Spanish weren't so hard for me. I'm taking first year. It's kind of embarrassing."

"You are on your way, then." She got up from the couch and went around to a file cabinet on the opposite wall to fish through some papers. "My job, Violet, is to take what is true about Violet Paz and put it into the *fiesta*. The *quinceañero* is a statement, about who you are and where you are going."

"How am I supposed to know that?"

"You do; you don't think you do, but you do. Who knows you better than yourself?" She brought a folder and the Snoopy notebook and sat back down next to me, flipping to the theme page in my notebook. " 'All the World's a Stage.' You are already cultivating one of your—not 'half,' but shall we say, hidden, or amateur, talents."

I relaxed some. What she said was smart. And she seemed interested in the me-ness of me. That was a new one. *I* wasn't even that interested in me.

Flora produced a questionnaire from her folder to fill out. "I'll be talking with you more in depth over the next few months. Now I want you to go see Fauna about your dress. Here," she said, handing Abuela's note back. "Give her this."

She smiled warmly. "You're going to have a fabulous *quince,* Violet. Think about what we've talked over, and I'll see you again in a month or so. Fauna will schedule you."

I let Fauna take my measurements and told her that, yes, I did like the fabric and the colors of the Chez Doll dress. I didn't tell her it was the dress part I disliked. I was beginning to feel like a freak.

After a perfunctory look through her heavy lenses at the white and purple gown, Fauna rewrapped it in its tissue paper and returned the box to me.

"Don't you need to . . . trace the pattern or something?" I asked.

A smile passed over her face. *"Todo está aquí,"* she said, pointing to her right temple.

"Cool," I said. Fauna had hidden talents too. I thought maybe I should tell her we didn't really know the Pope.

Then I thought, Nah.

17

The speech tournament at Taylor Park was approaching. On the day of my rehearsal with Mr. Soloman, I awoke to the familiar seesawing between blind courage and pure terror that preceded any performance. I was so revved up that I wore two different socks, one fuzzy anklet and one crew—both white, but still.

"Relax," Mr. Soloman said to me from a seat in the back row of one of the classrooms. "But not too much. Being keyed up keeps you on your toes."

I was already performing mental pirouettes. I'd waltz right through, then.

"We'll let you get your feet wet this weekend, and after that we'll work on revising and improving," he said.

Revising? I'd *finished* the writing part. And it was pretty darn good, if I said so myself, which I humbly kept quiet about. I paused to get in character, then began the routine I'd practiced a dozen times in front of my bedroom mirror.

I started out: "The story you are about to hear is true. None of the names have been changed, because no one is innocent. This is the sad case of a girl wrongfully accused, tried, and sentenced to life—with her family.

"It all began innocently enough: I was born, I went to kindergarten, I lost my front teeth. By then, it was already too late. I was a Paz."

I described my family's hereditary fashion deficiency, the domino gene, the penchant for puns. Then I narrated the crazy domino party, from Abuela's suspicious good luck to the conga line and the burning roast. Finally, the cops showed up.

"I can explain everything, Officers," I said, holding out my hands to accept the cuffs. "Just take me away, please!"

After a whirlwind trial, I was sentenced to life in prison for belonging to such a notorious family. The ending bit was me, gripping the bars of an imaginary cell, contemplating my future confinement. My whole family shared the same cell.

"I know there's no hope of ever being released. But maybe," my character hoped, "just maybe, with my record for good behavior . . . they'll put me in solitary!" The end.

I only faltered a little at the beginning, and I

remembered nearly all my lines. Mr. Soloman gave me a hand and said, "A few more run-throughs and some practice on your focus, and you'll be ready for Saturday. Then we can see how you stack up against the competition."

I gave him a bogus confident smile. "You've heard of Seinfeld? Chris Rock? Rosie O'Donnell?"

My coach rubbed his chin. "Who're they?"

I nodded. "That's what the judges'll be saying when they see my act." I scooped my books together and got ready to go.

Mr. Soloman clapped me on the back. "I like your style, kid. Make sure you get a good night's sleep before the tournament. And practice like crazy. And—"

"I know, I know. Kick ass!"

Mr. Soloman squinted at me through his raccoon-style glasses. "I was just going to tell you to wear matching socks."

I gave him a withering look and jammed out of there.

★   ★   ★

I nearly ran past Clarence Williams.

"Hey, Violet!"

He was out in the hall with another Extemper, a serious-looking guy who said hi and bye and hurried away with a stack of *Newsweek*s.

"Doesn't he talk to females?" I asked.

"Greg doesn't talk to anybody when he's on a trail."

"Huh?"

"That's what he calls his train of thought, Extemp-wise. Mental flash cards. He just made me give him a topic, and now he's like a hound on the trail."

"What was the topic?"

He showed me some teeth. "U.S.-Israeli foreign policy, the early years."

"Sounds like a breeze."

"Yeah, no sweat."

Clarence seemed taller than he had before. Then I realized I'd never seen him standing. He had on jeans and a long-sleeved red Chicago Bulls T-shirt and cross-trainers that had been scrubbed their whitest with a toothbrush recently.

"I missed you at the last team meeting," I said. "What happened?"

"Dentist."

When he said it, I noticed how very white his teeth were. "What are you doing here? Don't you Extempers guys just practice in a dark closet with a tape recorder?"

He laughed. "You'd be surprised how much acting is involved. Mainly, it's composure. But for me, that's acting!"

I knew what he meant. "Yeah!" I laughed weakly. "I hope I don't melt into a puddle on the floor in front of the judges."

Clarence shook his head. "It's all in the attitude. You put on your game face. And don't forget the sugar cubes."

"Sugar cubes?"

"Just bring some. You'll see." He picked up his pack and the Extemp file box from the floor. "I've got practice with Axelrod now. I'll see you Saturday."

★　★　★

Indeed, he was the first person I saw at school on Saturday. At the crack of 7:30, we were the first two on the curb, waiting for the bus and the team to show up. Clarence wore a lightweight gray suit, double-breasted, plus a light pink shirt, silver tie, and shiny black shoes. In short, he was styling. I felt underdressed in khakis and a knit top.

By 7:45, Janell, Leda, and the rest of the team had materialized, plus Ms. Joyner and Mr. Soloman. "The Ax never attends the early tourneys," Clarence had explained, as though these were beneath the head coach. Mr. Soloman gave me a thumbs-up from the front of the bus, which I returned, glad he was along.

The bus was hushed as we crossed the Lincolnville city limits. We hit the expressway and drove awhile, past the famous lip-shaped Magikist sign near the airport, bound for the far suburbs they call "the land beyond O'Hare." One thousand nine hundred eighty-seven, I thought. I had started counting the number of times I passed the Magikist sign when I was, like, five.

Then kids started to go over their lines. But did they practice together? No. Those working on their delivery faced their reflections in the bus windows and rehearsed out loud, complete with hand gestures and facial expressions.

Soon a low babel of voices intertwined—some earnest, some grave, some in Brooklyn or French or Tennessee Williams Southern accents—rising and falling with an urgency born of fear and too little sleep the night before. Motorists who happened to glance at our bus that morning saw what must have resembled a rolling insane asylum for deranged thespians. If their car windows were open, they might have heard the odd "I have a dream" mixed with "Stella!"

But on board the bus, the speechies acted like this was normal, so I gave it a try. You can never memorize anything too well.

We pulled into the parking lot of Taylor Park High School, and my entire O.C. speech momentarily dematerialized from my mind. As we got off the bus and people greeted friends and pointed out old nemeses, the lines came floating back, and I frantically whispered my opening over and over again. Janell and Leda tried to tell me about some TV show they'd seen, but I shook them off.

"The story you are about to hear is true. The story you are about to hear is true. . . ."

They both looked at me like I was nuts, but I had already learned my lesson in the bus window. You can never memorize anything too well.

18

Teams formed little outposts in the Taylor Park High cafeteria, hunkering down with their folders and lunches until time for rounds to begin. I thought if you connected the dots between school clusters, you'd get a weird map of the entire Chicago suburbs.

The competition schedule and room numbers for the different events were scribbled in blue marker on poster boards displayed near the cafeteria door. I left my stuff with the coaches at the Tri-Dist table and went to check the schedule for Original Comedy. My first round began ... right away! In five minutes! Depending on the event, rounds were staggered. Leda had an early round too, but

Janell's didn't start for an hour. I would have a whole two hours and fifteen minutes to get nervous before my second round. I saw that my O.C. teammate, Vera Campbell, would be in that round with me. Or against me.

How did this team thing work again?

I dashed back to the table for my folder and was about to bolt for the door when Clarence stepped in front of me.

"Sorry, Clarence—I've gotta go! My first round's in . . . three minutes! And I don't know where anything is!"

Clarence, looking cool and composed in his gray suit, took both my shoulders in his hands. "Take a deep breath, Violet. What's your room number?"

"Two-fourteen."

He let go. "That's upstairs, third door on your left."

I looked at him with openmouthed wonder.

"My brothers, remember? Years of competition." He grinned and fished in his suit pocket, placing a small, square object in my palm. A sugar cube. "For a boost, right before your round."

I stared at him. I'd forgotten about the sugar cubes. "Thanks," I whispered. Then I ran for the stairs.

★　★　★

"The story you are about to hear is true. . . . The story you are about to hear is true. . . ." I stuck the sugar cube in my mouth. Yuck. Mom would kill me if she knew I was eating pure, unadulterated sugar, without even any food coloring to dilute it.

"Violet Paz," called a man as I slipped into a seat near the back of Room 214. About a dozen kids I didn't know sat there quietly already.

"Here," I said.

The judge didn't continue the roll call. "Okay, Violet. You're on," he prompted.

Now?

I rose and forced myself to walk slowly to the front of the room. A lectern and a transparency projector had been pushed aside to create a few square feet of stage. Facing the audience, I dropped my eyes and took a breath. Then I made eye contact and began.

"The story you are about to hear is true. None of the names have been changed, because no one is innocent. . . ."

My mind raced at first—probably from the sugar cube—but when I found myself nailing my lines, I sort of let go. Used the Force. I even heard a laugh during the police scene, though I couldn't tell where it came from.

"Maybe, just maybe . . . they'll put me in solitary confinement!"

I held my gaze steady, then dropped it.

The applause came. Well, scattered clapping from a dozen sleepy people. That was good enough for me. I sat down.

"Way to go," came a whisper from behind me. I turned to find Janell cheering me on; it was okay to visit other people's rounds in between your own.

I nodded at her. A warm glow returned, and it wasn't the sugar cube this time.

We kicked back and watched the rest of the O.C.s. It felt great to have mine over and done with, especially when I watched a tense guy with curly blond hair and an ill-fitting three-piece suit rock back and forth as he spoke, trying to physically force the lines out. His routine was about driver's ed, only it wasn't funny. The only laughs came when he popped a button on his vest.

Among a few more unmemorable shticks, one guy named George somebody made everyone laugh, and you could tell some of the competitors tried hard not to. He did a spoof of a radio talk show, called "Dr. Speak Easy," in which he did the voices of all the callers plus the crackpot psychologist host.

"He's good," Janell said to me afterward, walking down the hall.

"Too good," I agreed.

"But you were right up there."

★ ★ ★

Mr. Soloman was holding the fort at our cafeteria table. "How'd it go?"

I smiled. "Pretty good, Coach. I got a laugh."

He beamed back. "That's how Johnny Carson got started."

I didn't feel like sitting still. Janell wanted to rehearse before her turn, so I polished off my half-empty bottle of juice and left to wander the halls.

Speechies roamed alone and in small knots, muttering lines or talking boisterously to one another:

"This tournament's running ahead of schedule."

"I know you from somewhere. What's your name? I'm one of Trish's friends. . . ."

"Something in the lockers smells like bad b.o.!"

I moved past a storage room labeled EXTEMP PREP with a construction-paper sign. Those who had drawn their topics were sequestered inside. Not a sound slipped from behind the closed door, its square window emitting a glare of fluorescent light. Outside, two white-shirted Extempers argued.

"Invariably, I'm wrong if I take a stance," said one of them.

"But remain objective and you've got no point," complained the other, a girl dressed just like the guys, in suit pants and tie, the latter of which she fiddled with tellingly.

I smiled; composure was an act for everyone, not just Clarence.

When I saw someone else from my team, we waved or gave each other the I-know-you look. I peeked into one of the duet rounds through the window in the door and could tell by the cadence and volume of the performers' voices that it was a humorous piece. Duet looked like fun; maybe shared stage fright was easier to take. I realized that, luckily, I hadn't had time to fall apart before my O.C., thanks to being called first. That was good to know.

Janell had asked me not to go to her rounds; she wasn't ready for an audience yet.

"But what about the judge and all the other Verse kids?"

She wrinkled her nose and said, "It's different when it's someone you know."

For me, it's strangers, but I wasn't about to argue with her. Everyone has their own stuff.

Janell and I rendezvoused with Leda during the lunch break. From the noise in the cafeteria, it sounded like everybody was full of adrenaline. Or sugar cubes. Leda and Janell said their rounds had been scary, and they didn't think they'd done very well. "Even though," Leda added, "mine *was* the best oration."

Clarence didn't show for lunch, but neither did the other Extempers from our team. I saw Ms. Joyner carry three brown-bag lunches in the direction of the prep room, and that mystery was solved.

I chewed my own cheese sandwich, though my taste buds would have no recollection of the event, and opened a bottle of sparkling water.

"Tut, tut," Leda tutted at me. "Wrong brand, darling." She jerked her head at a nearby table where everyone was drinking from liters of Evian.

I'd seen kids carrying them through the halls between rounds, cradled like infants. "What school is that?" I asked.

"Evian High," Janell dubbed it, and we cracked up.

★　★　★

I felt pretty good going into Round Two, even had time to saunter casually up to my room, 215, which I figured would be right next to 214.

Wrong. Next to Room 214 was the guys' bathroom, and next to that were a bunch of locked offices. I ran the length of the building to the other end of the hall and arrived, dripping, just as the O.C. judge asked a student to shut the door.

All eyes in the room locked on me as I slid past her and into a seat.

"Violet Paz?" called the judge.

Incredible. And I didn't have another sugar cube.

I walked to the front, feeling a sweatball roll down my back, paused, and began.

I seemed to be a step behind my routine all the way through. My lines were shakier. I messed up the domino part and skipped the conga line, so the roast catching on fire didn't make any sense and the cops showing up seemed tacked on to the ending. Then I stumbled over the last line, and when I finished, the audience wasn't sure it was over. I practically had to say "the end" before they dismissed me with their cold-fish clapping.

My heart sank into my stomach during the other performances. As a double insult, my teammate Vera went on right after me and did great. Vera was dressed in her Sunday best, including stockings and pumps, which seemed overblown until you saw her act. The costume fit right in with her one-woman monologue, a diatribe by an aged "Miss Sippy," a country transplant to the city who rails on every aspect of Chicago life but refuses to leave. Miss Sippy was blunt, but she managed to evoke the cold reality of a wait at the bus stop in a January blizzard and the smell of the subway that comes up through the city sidewalk vents in July. Her stock complaint was: "You call that livin'?"

The sketch ended with Miss Sippy deciding to move back to the country, until she heard there was no bus service there. "No CTA? I got to get to all the places I can't stand to be in. No CTA? You call that livin'?"

She brought the house down, which was a tall order for ten kids in dress clothes and a teacher playing judge on her day off. Even the girl in the third row from Evian High was laughing. Vera got a huge hand.

"Good going," I said to her afterward, meaning it. I was

really glad The Ax had chosen comedy for me. If I had to lose to somebody, it was nice to be able to laugh while they were beating me.

★　★　★

When the final-round postings appeared in place of the earlier schedules, I was crushed. Neither Vera nor I was included. Only two of our team members made finals, Zeno Clark and Greg Ibarra, Clarence's Extemp buddy.

The Extemporaneous Speaking final was closed to spectators, district rules, so most of us crowded into Zeno's final round. This year, The Ax had him working on a scene from a new version of *Dracula*.

Zeno's Dracula was extremely creepy in his normalcy, and nobody else had picked such a cool excerpt. We weren't surprised to hear Zeno called to take the Dramatic Interp trophy at the awards ceremony, a casual affair that took place on a portable riser in a corner of the cafeteria. A few cheers went up, rules notwithstanding, and mine was one of them. Greg Ibarra came in sixth, or last of the finalists in Extemp, but we all clapped just as hard for him. Dr. Speak Easy won the O.C. event.

Forestfield High School took the team trophy; they'd had six finalists. Leda punched me when all six of them trooped up to accept the trophy, raising their water bottles in victory.

"Evian High!" she said with disgust.

So this was how losing felt.

The lump in my stomach settled in for the long haul as our team headed for the bus. I forgot to count the Magikist sign on the way home.

19

My critiques from the judges varied. I had placed third out of nine in my first round, and the judge had remarked on the sheet, "Good topic—original! How about some more dialogue?"

In my bumbling second performance, I'd come in seventh. There had only been seven O.C.s. That meant I was worse than the guy who'd spoofed a television wrestling match, and nobody had laughed at him. The judge's suggestion to me? "Try to memorize your lines."

Yes, I would. Yes, I would.

Mr. Soloman possessed the good grace to say only,

"Next time, girl," on our way off the bus. I figured he was saving the yelling for later.

So I was feeling low when I got home and slouched into the kitchen through the side door. Mom sat at the table, writing, while Chucho stood at his bowl, chunking down his dry food without chewing.

"How'd you do, hon?" Mom asked me, not taking her eyes off her notebook. She was working on restaurant plans again.

"Okay," I said. "I came in third." Which was true, sort of.

"That's nice . . ." She finished the sentence she was writing and set her WBEZ pen down. "How about this one, Violet? I was up all night thinking about it: a drive-through bakery specializing in breads." She paused, waiting for me to ask.

"Let me guess. 'A Moveable Yeast'?"

"Close, but no cigar. I call it 'Catch 'er in the Rye'!" She waited a beat. *"HA!"* she prompted, and when I didn't join in, she gave three halfhearted shakes.

These titles were getting so bad, she should've been naming hair salons. I said as much, then wished I could immediately take it back when Mom replied, "Hmmm. D'you think so?"

I threw up my hands. "Who cares what the theme is? If you'd ever stick to one thing, Mom, maybe you'd actually *open* a restaurant."

Bold words directed at my *quince* captain of strategy. But Mom wasn't mad. She cut her eyes at me, and this time

I saw her hypothetical plans fall in one swoop, like a house of cards. After my devastating theatrical loss, I just couldn't leave it at that.

"Plans aren't everything, Mom," I said, and left the kitchen.

★ ★ ★

The seasons had changed. September had given us a final warm clap on the back and let the screen door bang on its way out. October stirred a familiar stew of drizzle and autumn leaves. In neighboring Wisconsin, bold flaxen, persimmon, and cherry-colored foliage drew dull Illinois drones like hungry bees. But here on my corner of Woodtree Lane, all the leaves had turned a sallow yellow and threatened to drop with the next breeze.

Chucho enjoyed the wet and decay of the sparse piles that drifted up against the curbs on our daily walks, while I was just a shuffling lump on the other end of the leash. I kicked limply at the brown and yellow curls on the sidewalk, biding my time until the first snowfall, and the ones after that. To ski, or not to ski.

For now, it was speech season. I had to tell Mom no when she asked if I wanted to drive up to the Wisconsin Dells with her and a friend on Saturday to look at the trees, because of rehearsal. Vera Campbell and I were supposed to coach each other, and I heard that all the Extempers would be there too, working on their files. This interested Leda enough that she was going to skip a lucrative Greenpeace event to come to school.

I knew I'd have plenty to do. Following the Taylor Park

tournament, Mr. Soloman had videotaped my routine and sat me down in C206 in front of a television to dissect it.

The agony.

Now I knew why some actors refuse to watch their own movies. My six-and-a-half-minute performance took on all the hallmarks of the Chinese water torture: There I stood, blabbing on and on about my boring family, managing to make even the conga line and the burning roast seem boring. How could I ever have thought any of this was funny? By the time I begged the police to take me away, please, the audience must have heaved a huge sigh of relief.

Mr. Soloman just left the tape running and looked at me through his glasses.

"I . . . guess you had to be there?" I mumbled.

He thought a moment.

"I guess *you* had to be there." He motioned for me to get out of my seat and led me down front.

"Violet, remember when I showed you that sea ostrich speech on tape?"

I nodded. That one was starting to look good in retrospect.

"What was it that we both agreed was wrong with that piece?"

Our conversation came floating back to me. "Too much narration. The guy never gave any other point of view but his own."

Mr. Soloman nodded. "I think that's what we're seeing here."

I felt the stab of truth, then a flash of anger. He could have told me this sooner. "Then why'd you let me compete with it?"

He smiled at me like Glinda the Good Witch. "You had to learn it on your own. Now, forget about last week. Watch me."

I moved back a few paces, and he began my speech. Knew the lines better than me: "The story you are about to hear is true," he deadpanned. At the end of the intro, he stopped. "Here is where you make the big shift. The monotone works to draw the audience in with mock seriousness. Then you want to surprise them—wow them—with your first character. Now, your turn."

"You mean, *do* the characters?"

He nodded again. "You've got all the funny elements in there, Violet. Bring them out."

I improvised a dialogue between Abuela and Marianao, changing my voice for each character.

"Not bad," Mr. Soloman said, stopping me. "But think *big*. Exaggerate the hand motions. Throw in an imaginary prop or two. And don't look at me when you're in character—pick your focal points. Try it again," he commanded.

This time I had Abuela do a little dance around an imaginary Chucho, who was trying to eat the buckles off her imaginary shoes, and I threw in Marianao's cigar.

I looked up to find Mr. Soloman laughing. Hard.

When I finished, he was still smiling. "That cigar! Did you make that up?"

"Uh, yeah," I lied, a narcotic glow spreading through me. I was starting to feel like I'd do anything for a laugh, it felt that good. I suddenly understood comedy acts like the Three Stooges, and Abbott and Costello. Even the film *Dumb and Dumber* took on a new sheen; no wonder Jeff Daniels and Jim Carrey had done it.

"That's great," Mr. Soloman said.

He walked me through the rest of my routine, making suggestions here and there. Pantomiming the conga line was a challenge, but I was beginning to see the light. Be funny. Why hadn't I thought of that before?

My great brainstorm hit as we were wrapping up for the day. Mr. Soloman had said to take what I knew about how competition rounds worked and apply it to my presentation. I remembered how deathly quiet the classrooms had been during rounds. If I could shock the audience out of that silent cocoon, I'd get people's attention, all right.

"Hey, Mr. S.! Remember that Superbaby routine? How the guy starts out with that horrible baby cry?"

"Yeah. So?"

"What about . . . if I do something like that? I could have the police chase me up to the stage!"

"With a siren blaring," he put in. "That would really tie your theme together—sentenced to life!" He unplugged the video monitor and started winding up its cord. "Work on it, and show me next time. Rolling Fields tourney is in two weeks."

"Who's on first?" I asked, hoping it would be me.

"Huh?"

"No, Huh's on second, Who's on first," I said, jogging up the ramp between the tiers of seats. "See you next Tuesday, Mr. S.!"

I slowly added ideas to the *quince* notebook. The big day was on a Sunday. While we weren't inviting anyone to a special church service, Mom and Dad and I had decided our family would attend regular Mass at St. Edna's that morning, for posterity, and then get ready for the party. I had nearly finalized the lineup for the "All the World's a Stage" show:

5 pm—Guests arrive, sign guestbook, find seats
5:30—Janell introduces V.; entrance; presented to
        Dad; dance together
    Hors d'oeuvres served
    Janell's poetry presentation
    A medley of Broadway show tunes by V. on piano
    Leda's speech (?)
    Interpretive dance solo by Janell
    V.'s comedy speech
6 pm—Dinner served; band begins
7 pm—Cake presentation
7:30—Guest dancing

That ought to do it. By the time the party was over, I'd be a woman. Or at least I hoped so, for Abuela's sake. I showed my *damas* the outline one day after school as we hung out by Janell's locker.

"I'm supposed to give my speech?" Leda asked, surprised. She and Janell had received mixed reviews at the tourney too. "You want 'Plows, Not Cows'?"

"This isn't a rally," Janell remarked.

"Yeah, can you try and come up with something to go with 'All the World's a Stage'?"

"And not 'All the World's a Cage,' either," warned Janell. "Guests will be eating meat, and we don't want to freak them out."

"Yeah," I said, "we're serving some of those bacon-grease ice cream cones, and we want everybody to enjoy them."

Leda clapped steely eyes on me. "*Don't* mention that."

Janell fought to keep her trembling lips in a straight line.

"Sorry," I lied.

Leda ignored me as she cranked up the gears and pulleys in her head. She was on a trail, as the Extempers called it. "I'll think of something," she mused. "After last week, I might try another event. Declamation, maybe. At least Dec speeches are written by somebody else."

"Well, hurry up. I've only got another six months before I'm supposed to be a woman."

Leda eyed my still sunken chest. "You'd better start exercising, then."

20

When Vera and I met on Saturday afternoon to rehearse, we found an invitation taped to the door of Room C206. In wiggly, scary-type letters, the sign read, "ARE YOU AFRAID OF THE DARK? Scared of screams? Terrified by great food, music, and costume judging? Come to BOO FEST, at Zeno Clark's. Saturday, Halloween Night. After dark. All Speechies welcome."

"Cool," I said. "Are you going?"

Vera looked at me with hungry dark eyes. "You know it. I love costume parties! It'll be right after the Rolling Hills tourney, and everybody's gonna be there. You just won't know who's who." She broke into a broad grin.

"That's the part I like. Me and Cherise already have our costumes."

Vera was a compact girl, as short as me but with definition—hips, bust, even her shoulders were more rounded and pronounced, her face contoured under a mellow cocoa complexion. She wore her straightened shoulder-length hair pulled back, or up, or to the side in interesting configurations. But her identifying feature was her posture. She had this *stance,* like a cat ready to spring. I thought I'd probably be able to spot her in any guise.

"What are you going as?"

"That's for me to know, and you not to find out."

"We'll see," I said.

Miss Sippy and I performed our speeches for each other and then made comments about what was funny and what wasn't, where things could be speeded up or slowed down, and how the performance might look from a judge's point of view. Then we got down to the good stuff.

"Who do you think has the best O.C. so far?"

Vera thought. "There's two or three that are gonna give everybody trouble."

"Dr. Speak Easy?"

"He's good, but not that good. Nah, there's a girl, she's from that school where they all carry those water bottles around?"

"Evian High!" I said. "I think I saw her."

"She does an absolute, dead-ringer impression of those dumb-blonde infomercial chicks. No offense," Vera added.

I shrugged.

"And then there's a guy, he's *so* annoying, who does this

rap about dating the ugliest girl in school. 'Mary Ann Pimpleberry,' he calls it. His name was Guy something. He did the same O.C. last year, so he's really got it down. But that seems like cheating."

"And who's the third contender?"

Vera shot me a look. "Me, girl! You better watch out!"

Touché.

I smiled. "You've got my vote," I said.

Vera turned serious. "Don't worry about me, Vi. You just go in there and kick some serious Rolling Hills butt, okay?"

"Promise," I agreed, and we gave each other a closed-fist handshake. "You too."

★   ★   ★

Afterward, a few of us hung around the front hallway waiting for rides. As I mindlessly ran through my new lines, Clarence said, "Hey, Violet. Do your O.C. for us, will you?"

"Yeah," said Leda. "We'll critique it."

"No," countered Clarence. "Just for fun."

So I did.

I couldn't have asked for a more suck-up audience. Besides them all being on my team, they were slaphappy from several hours of extracurricular concentration. Everybody laughed.

On our way outside, Clarence fell in step with me.

"That was really something, Violet. You're so creative! Did you just make all that up?"

I shook my head. "Most of it really happened. Sort of."

"You mean, your family is like that?"

"Pretty much."

"Sounds like fun."

"Living with them? It's—a challenge."

"I'd like to meet them sometime," he said sincerely.

"What?" My stomach squirmed. I dropped my folder, and a bunch of English handouts fell to the damp ground, soaking up old rain like dishrags. They tore as Clarence and I picked them up.

I stood there with the ripped, wet papers in my hands as Clarence leapt to his feet.

"Well, bye. I gotta go!" He ran for a car at the curb.

I opened my mouth, but no sound came out. I watched him go. Then I went to catch a ride home with Leda.

★ ★ ★

The week crawled by. Wednesday, after my piano lesson, I took Chucho for his walk and read a little bit of the Jean Ferris novel I'd checked out of the school library. I was thinking of maybe getting around to doing my Spanish homework when Dad stuck his head in my room and called me to the phone. He was working the graveyard shift at the pharmacy that month and was just waking up. He had on a faded striped pajama top and green paisley bottoms, plus a pair of Mom's slippers decorated to look like duck feet.

"*Buenos días,* Dad," I said to him with a straight face, and dashed downstairs to the kitchen phone.

"Hello?"

"Violet." The voice poured like liquid velvet from the receiver. No, it sounded more like—what was a strong wood? Oak? Like velvet oak.

"Violet," it repeated. Whose voice was it?

"It's Clarence."

"Oh, yeah, sure. Hi," I said. His voice sounded—richer over the phone.

Uncomfortable Pause Number One.

"Um, how did you get my number?" I demanded, combing my brain for any discussion topic and coming up with a winner.

"There's this invention called a phone book," he said, and I could hear the soft smile in his voice, picture those smooth lips slightly parted in an intimate grin.

The language generator in my brain shut down.

"Is it okay to call you there?" he asked politely when I didn't answer. "Violet?"

Form. Words. "Oh, sure! Not a problem," I managed.

Another uncomfortable pause. And we're both speechies! If it was this hard for us to converse, other people must just grunt and bang the receiver on their heads.

I made a colossal effort to mold a conversation out of these words and silences. "So, Clarence." That was a start. "Are you ready for the Rolling Hills tourney?"

"I'm always ready," he said with customary assurance. His game face, he called it. "But that's not why I'm calling."

"What's up?"

"I was wondering if you're going to Zeno's party on Saturday."

"The Halloween party?"

"Yeah, the Clarks throw one every year. Zeno's older brother was an Extemp champ, Sully Clark. He's off at Dartmouth. But my brothers always go if they're in town."

"So, are *you* going?" Another stellar question.

"I am. And you?"

Now we were getting somewhere. "I—yeah, sure, I'm going," I said, deciding it then and there.

"I guess I'll see you at the party then. Just thought I'd ask, since we won't get a chance to see each other much at the tourney, and I hardly ever run into you in the halls. So . . . I'll talk to you later."

"Wait! What'll you be wearing?"

I heard his easy chuckle. "It'll be a surprise."

I hung up, wondering, Did he just ask me on a date? But no, it couldn't be a date. He didn't invite me; we were only meeting there. And we might not even be able to recognize each other. I may not have been a social whirlwind, but I knew that even blind dates finally actually *meet.* Was there another type of date, even further removed than a blind date?

Halloween. It would have to be a headless date.

21

Now I'd have to totally reinvent myself with a great Halloween costume; people sounded serious about the masquerade aspect of Zeno's party. And what with the *quince* party plans and comedy speech, my artistic reserves were running low. I supposed next someone would ask me to repaint the Sistine Chapel. With my elbows.

Instead, bright and early Monday morning—that is, *lunes por la mañana*—my Spanish teacher laid a semester project on us.

As Leda and I savored our last few moments of freedom in the hallway, Señora Wong summoned us to class with a glare. We were learning Spanish from a woman who didn't even need language to communicate. Wasn't that a conflict of interest?

"*Presentaciones sobre la cultura hispánica,*" she wrote on the board, underlining it with squeaky chalk. "Hispanic culture presentations. Groups of two, ten minutes apiece, on whichever Spanish-speaking country interests you most. Accompanied by a paper, five to eight pages, *en inglés.*" She wrote the due date on the board, the week of *diciembre 5.* "Using at least three separate references, I want you to research the music, literature, food, or some other cultural aspect of your country. Bring something to share with the *clase,* a treat, a song–"

"Can we bring tacos?" somebody shouted.

"Tacos are fine," the good *señora* said, nodding. "But most importantly," she said, looking directly at me, for some reason, "be *creativo.*"

★ ★ ★

By the end of the day, Leda had already plotted the whole thing out. "Paz!" She grabbed me firmly by one arm after the last bell rang and led me to a doorway where we wouldn't be trampled. "We have to give Señora Doble-U our topics next week, and this time, *chica,* we've got this puppy in the bag."

I didn't see a semester project as a puppy, nor did I think it would fit in any bag, but I let her tell me why.

"*¿Por qué?*" Leda rubbed her white-blond head with both hands, as if this would increase the flow of blood to my brain. "Paz. Get it? Spanish-speaking culture. Your dad: Spanish speaking. He tells us what we need to know, we write it down and tack on a couple of sources. End of semester project, A plus."

She looked incredulous that I didn't jump on this gift.

"*¿Qué es el* problem-*o?*"

"*El problema,*" I mumbled. "Dad and I don't–speak Spanish together, I told you."

"This'll be in English, that's the beauty of it. Now, what'll it be, art, food, music? The land of Cuba awaits you."

"Island," I muttered.

"Huh?"

"It's an *island,*" I said, "not a land."

"Whatever, Paz. What it is, is an easy ticket to a quick A in Spanish. Does that not sound alluring to you?"

Easy ticket, quick A. "Well, yeah . . ."

"That's more like it. Your dad's into music, isn't he? I'm into world beat, but I haven't done Cuba yet. Talk to him, okay?"

So I agreed. But I made her come with me.

Dad was on morning shift now. He hated all the shift changes but never got around to looking for a job at another pharmacy. When we got home, Leda and I found him lounging in the family room in his neatly creased sweatpants, just as he was sliding his yellow-socked feet into his maroon slipper-shoes.

As we'd planned, Leda was the one to put the touch on him. Her tone was abjectly humble. When she asked if he could find it in his heart to "please mentor this important project," Dad puffed out his chest under a lavender polo shirt that most men his age wouldn't be caught dead in and said, "Sure. I'd love to."

I stared at him, but not because of the shirt. I was used

to that. I wasn't used to hearing him say he'd love to talk about Cuban music, or life on the island, or anything about Cuba—which he just had.

"I'll give you a few tapes and a cigar for your show-and-tell," he even offered.

"It's not show-and-tell, Dad," I snapped.

"No," he said with a grin, not noticing my mood. "More like hear-and-smell. *HA!*" He gave Mom's laugh, not bothering with the beats.

"Dad, y'know, cigars and the cha-cha are not going to cut it with our teacher. That's all people already know about Cuba." It was all *I* knew.

He and Leda were still smiling at his joke. "What else do you need to know, Violet? What about all that history I told you?"

Had I missed a decade somewhere?

"What! Dad, all you ever say about Cuba's past is that Batista was a real bastard." Dad's smile ran down like an old battery. "You never even made it to Castro!" Not in English, anyway.

He had no answer for that. While I flashed my eyes at him, Leda put in, "I guess we'll have to do mambo, then."

Dad threw her a grateful look. *"Sí,"* he said, not returning my gaze. "We'll do mambo."

★   ★   ★

Leda and I practiced "Plows, Not Cows" and what Mr. Soloman had dubbed "The Loco Family" for each other out on the porch, with one of Abuelo's discarded tapes playing in the background; my grandfather had upgraded to CD years ago.

"This is nice and everything," Leda said as the last song played. "But can you understand a word they're saying?"

I cocked my head. "I heard *amor*..."

"And *pata*–what's that again?"

"Foot, I believe."

We looked at each other quizzically.

I sighed. "I'll try to get some more information out of Dad."

She put on her jacket. "See you tomorrow."

I went downstairs and found my father, still in the family room, reading a copy of *Golf World*. I plopped onto the couch next to his chair.

"*Eh,* Violeta. *¿Qué te pasa?*" He closed the magazine.

"It's those tapes, Dad. We're supposed to write a little talk to give, and we don't know what to say. Can't you tell me about the styles of Cuban music, or the history behind it all?"

Dad colored. "*Pues,* those are not really my tapes. . . . They're before my time." He twisted *Golf World* into a telescope, peered through it, put it down. "I like to listen to them every now and then, but I'm not up on the music like your *abuelo* is. You could ask him . . . but he and Mami just left on a cruise for their anniversary."

"I don't have much time. We're looking for something more modern, anyway. We have to show sources for our topic by the end of next week. Don't you have a book or something?"

"I'll tell you what. Now is the time for your *tía* Luci to come to the rescue. Why don't you give her a call?"

Incredible. He was weaseling out again. "Dad! Hello,

it's me. Your daughter, Violet? Isn't there a single thing you can tell me about Cuban music?"

He went pink again, let out his breath. "Well, no, not really. See, I didn't listen to that stuff when I was growing up." He fiddled with the magazine in his lap. "I listened to rock and roll–the Rolling Stones, Clapton, Led Zeppelin. . . . Papi's music?" He rolled his eyes. "It embarrassed me. Like, I'd roll up the car window if Papi's radio station was too loud when we stopped at a stoplight."

"Oh."

"Only now I kind of like to listen to it."

The way I like to listen to his music sometimes. "I'll give Tía a call, Dad." I slid my eyes sideways at him. "Hey? And if I find out any information, I'll let you know."

He grinned and uncrumpled his magazine. "I could learn something, *¿no?*"

"It's possible." I sat back against the cushions as Mom and Chucho joined us.

Mom looked tired; Friday is a busy day for thrift. I asked her if she could drive me to school to catch the tournament bus in the morning.

"On one condition," she said, settling Chucho on her lap. He yawned, gave a little squeak, and closed his eyes.

"What's that?"

"Well, I haven't seen your speech yet. I've been meaning to ask if you'd do it for your father and me."

Dad put *Golf World* down again. "*Sí,* Violet. Let's see the speech."

Another command performance. Suddenly, I was much more nervous than I'd been at the first tournament.

I didn't have to live with anyone from that audience. But Mom's and Dad's eyes were trained on me. I wasn't going to pass up this opportunity.

I tested out my new beginning on them, making them jump, and wound my way through the speech. Mom started laughing early on– *"HA!"*–but I didn't let her throw me. Dad kept up a rolling chuckle as I did my impression of his relatives one by one, and by the end they were both howling. Only Chucho was silent.

"¡Brava!" cried Dad.

"That was wonderful, honey," Mom said, smiling.

"Of course," said Dad, "people are going to think we are a little bit crazy. . . ."

Mom looked at him crossways. "If the shoe fits, Albert."

I held my breath.

He relaxed, and they both chuckled.

Sure, they are my parents and all, and they're supposed to cheer me on. But it felt good. I went up to my room with a warm swelling in my chest–or was it in my head? Either way, I was nearly ready for the tourney.

22

*J*ust like every year, I couldn't think of a decent Halloween costume. I would end up throwing together something from the thrift shop as usual. Why was it so hard to be creative on demand? The speech coaches expected us to just scribble up a little old speech, perform as if we'd been doing it for years, and win. So did Abuela, in a way. And Señora Doble-U thought she could wring blood from a stone: "Be *creativo.*"

On Tuesday when I got home from rehearsal, I decided to do the most uncreative thing I could think of: watch TV. I popped a bowl of popcorn and got my book for the commercial breaks. Then I went downstairs to watch some junky reruns. Entering the family room, I was assailed by the whine of an electric drill and my brother's muffled mutters emanating from beneath his Cubs hat. I looked forward to seeing Mark's head again, once baseball-cap season ended with the World Series. It looked like it would be Atlanta on top again this year.

Mark sat in Dad's avocado-colored vinyl recliner, with a bucket of golf balls at his feet. On a folded newspaper atop the matching avocado vinyl footstool, he was drilling holes in the balls, one by one. He stopped to stretch out a palm for some popcorn.

"Dad's gonna kill you," I said, giving Mark about six kernels, which he inhaled.

"I'm not hurtin' the furniture."

"You'll wake him up, then."

"Will not."

"Yes, you will, Mark."

"He's not here," Mark said with satisfaction, and his drill bit poked through the golf ball and into the newspaper below. He lifted the paper to show me that the footstool remained intact.

I stared at him. Was this kid charmed, or what? "What are you doing anyway?"

"Making my Halloween costume. I had to do something with these balls."

"And what are you making exactly?"

"Mom's going to sew them all over my old Batman costume, and, check it out! Golf Ball Man!"

I had to hand it to him. That was a pretty good idea.

Weird. And original. He could safely say that no one else would be wearing that one.

I gave up on watching TV—it was too noisy—and took my popcorn up to my room. For once, I appreciated my little brother's weirdness. Fueled by the specter of Golf Ball Man, I decided to go through my closet and see if there was any costume material I had overlooked.

There wasn't. But I did find some decent clothes to wear to the Rolling Hills tournament on Saturday: my blue power suit. That's what Mom called it, crisp cerulean-blue pants with a puffy-sleeved jacket to match. The jacket had four huge black buttons down the front that made it—powerful. And me, in it. I wore it to church at St. Edna's once, and it was hard to sit, stand, and kneel sedately.

I remembered feeling underdressed at the last tourney, even though there had been plenty of kids in casual pants and shirts. Clarence and Vera, in their Sunday or weekday best, seemed to grab an edge in their rounds. In speech events with no costume requirement, dress was indeed crucial. So I did the unthinkable.

I ironed my power suit.

Dad had come home, and he gasped when he found me in a corner of the family room, iron in hand. "Job interview?" he asked.

I grinned. "Speech tournament."

He nodded approvingly. His clothing combinations may be unorthodox, but he's no slob. Dad irons everything, even velour. He dumped a pile of dress socks on the board as I hung up my blue suit. "*Y cómo va el eh*speech?"

"I think I'm getting better."

"Mejorar es mejor que nada," he said wisely. "Ah, you have an e-mail from your *abuela*. On my desk."

"Thanks. Uh, what did that mean, that thing in Spanish?"

"Hmmm? Oh, nothing," he said, frowning at the iron controls.

I set my lips. "There's no setting for 'sock,' Dad," I said, picking up the hanger with my suit on it and exiting, stage left.

Querida Nieta, the e-mail message read, **The cruise, it was wonderful. How is the school? It makes a long time that we don't talk, your Abuelo says HOLA. Mamita sends a hug. Listen, my dear, when will be the dress fitting? Let me know, because I have something very especial for you. Love y besos, Abuela**

Ugh, the dress. All the rest of the ceremony, I thought I could handle. It was time to face my fears. I decided to give Señora Fauna a call. Flora answered the telephone and said she'd just been thinking about me. She gave an animated account of my party design, detailing everything from the *Playbill* look-alike invitations to the red carpet and rental chandeliers.

Fauna had good news for me too. My dress was ready to try on and measure for alterations, and similar styles could be fashioned for my *damas* at a reasonable price. But I should be sure to have them mention my name at the desk. I wondered if Señora Fauna, dressmaker to the party planner to the stars, had been a Secret Service agent in a past life.

Leda, Janell, and I all went for a fitting together with Mom. I was just thinking that it was a good thing Abuela wasn't here to start a Pink fight, when Fauna brought my "dress" out on a hanger and swirled it around in front of us. The skirt fabric was the familiar breezy white muslin, but not so sheer. Fauna had added purple velvet dot accents and a royal purple velvet bodice, delicately embroidered in a white curling-leaf pattern. But it wasn't a dress at all.

For once, my entourage allowed me into the fitting room by myself. I emerged and turned slowly in a circle in this whisper of a gown, really a costume out of *Cleopatra* or *The Arabian Nights,* with sheer cap sleeves, a tight purple bodice, and a long white billowy skirt that gathered tight at each ankle. Pants! Really good-looking pants.

I stared at Fauna and asked *Why? How?* with my hands. She went to her worktable and returned with a folded note. It was Abuela's note, the one I'd delivered. I recognized *por favor* and *vestido* and my name in her choppy handwriting, and next to it she'd sketched my outfit. Wow. I twirled around a few more times.

Señora Flora waltzed in for a look, and everyone agreed that Abuela's idea had turned out perfectly. Fauna would sew Janell's and Leda's gowns in different solid colors, in the same contrasting fabrics as mine. Janell picked an undersea green-gray shade and Leda a dusky rose from Fauna's swatches. Next–Flora checked her list–shoes and jewelry, followed by my first dance lesson.

I called Abuela in Miami as soon as I got home. "Abuela, the dress! It's gorgeous!"

"You like, no?" she said proudly.

"I like, I like. Was that the special something you promised me?"

"*Eh? Ah, eso.* No, Violet, something else is coming," she teased.

"Like what?"

"*Paciencia. Espérate.*"

Those words I knew. Similar to *mañana*—the way Dad says it, like tomorrow will never come—*espera* means "wait."

Meanwhile, pledges from my party sponsors continued to roll in. Mom received weekly updates from Abuela via e-mail; it looked as though we might end up with a *surplus* of money.

Dad's eyes lit up when Mom mentioned this. They dimmed when she said we'd have to return any extra cash.

I didn't care what they did with it. I'd passed the pink dress test. I might make it through Year Fifteen unscathed yet. Bonus-plus: My cast of *quince* characters, both on and off the stage, was seemingly under control, *and* I had a headless date for Halloween. Wonders would never cease.

23

The next morning, packing sugar cubes and this huge ego, I rode the team bus to Rolling Hills High and checked the O.C. board for my name. Sweet! Two early rounds, then a few hours to sit in on performances. And Janell had said I could come watch her.

On the way to my first round, Clarence slipped me a message on a ripped triangle of notebook paper. In square-lettered printing it said,

SEE YOU TONIGHT, C.

A strong chemical reaction took place inside me; I might have discovered a new element. I put the note in my jacket pocket for luck.

I was a little nervous about my lines since I'd changed so many, but my power suit got me through the door, and once again the sugar cube revved my engine and let me think ahead as I talked. Or at least it seemed that way.

The judge called me third, after two people I didn't know. The second girl spoke in such a mouse squeak that everyone had to lean forward to hear, and the applause afterward was aptly hushed. So the stage was set for my new entrance.

"Violet Paz?"

I waited a beat, two, three—until heads began to turn. Then I jumped out of my seat, shouting, "Stop! Police!" I ran for the front of the room, whooping my best rendition of a police siren at full volume.

I broke off in midcry and made eye contact with the crowd. "The story you are about to hear is true. None of the names have been changed, because no one is innocent. . . ."

I segued to the flashback: me, the narrator, playing straight man to me, my cousin Marianao *con cigarro*.

"Wha' ju mean, 'no *eh*smoking'?" my Marianao said with indignation. That is, me, doing a bad imitation of a Cuban with a bad accent. "I yam no *eh*smoking, cousin."

My narrator jammed hands on hips. "And just what would you call this?" I exaggerated huffs and puffs, wheezing a little.

The response? "Is the *cigarro* which is *eh*smoking. I only happen to be breathing on the other end."

Some laughs here. I took the audience by the hand and led them through my house, past my relatives, into the backyard. Then I became my grandfather.

"*¡Ay, ay, ay!* I am hot tonight, *como* Tito Puente. I am *el rey de los disc jockeys,* and king of the Weber!"

I pantomimed the conga line picking him up, a bit of body comedy that resembled a cross between a Russian dance and Pin the Tail on the Donkey. It worked. I heard actual giggles out there.

By the time I raised the noise level again with Abuelo's shouts, Chucho's howling, and another siren, the room was breaking up. I let the police lead me away to prison and brought the story in a neat circle, ending in my monotone, "Maybe they'll put me in solitary confinement. It would be a relief." I made eye contact again for punch, and dropped my head.

To thunderous applause.

★　★　★

Round Two went as well, and then I headed for Janell's second round. I didn't try to get her attention, just slipped in with the others and sat quietly across the room from her. She had told me earlier that she'd chosen the first poem especially to read at my *quince* party. She and Leda and I would begin rehearsals soon.

To my surprise, the round was pretty evenly mixed with girls and guys. I listened to four Verse programs—seemingly dozens of poems, all unfamiliar except for one Emily Dickinson that I vaguely recalled—and then the judge asked for Janell. Looking confident in a pale-yellow print dress that reached her ankles and displayed her usual clunky black boots, she glided up front. The woman was light on her feet. And thanks to the martial arts, I bet she could kill you with those shoes.

"Growing up"—she addressed the audience—"is a state of body and a state of mind. The two don't always mature together, and growth never really stops—it just slows down, until one day you find you're a"—hairsbreadth of a beat—"phenomenal woman. 'Phenomenal Woman,' a poem by Maya Angelou." My *quince* poem.

Phenomenal? Me? A fuzzy glow spread inward. I didn't know Janell cared so.

She recited in a voice near her own, but with a swing to it. " 'Pretty women wonder where my secret lies. / I'm not cute or built to suit a fashion / Model's size . . .' "

Hey, wait a minute. My glow tapered off.

" 'But when I start to tell them, / They think I'm telling lies. / I say, / It's in the reach of my arms, / The span of my hips, / The stride of my step, / The curl of my lips.' "

The glow fuzzed out. My hips and lips were nobody's business.

" 'I'm a woman / Phenomenally. / Phenomenal woman, / That's me.' "

I could just see Mark in his *quinceañero* tux, pointing at me and laughing in front of all our relatives, my friends, my piano teacher, and the Caprizios, whom Mom had insisted on inviting.

Janell let loose another string of body parts, repeating, " 'I'm a woman / Phenomenally. / Phenomenal woman, / That's me.' "

Oh, sure. With my stumpy legs and triple-*a* bra size, real phenomenal. What was that supposed to mean? The warm glow had turned to cold needles that I couldn't ignore.

Janell continued ruthlessly. " 'I say, / It's in the arch of my back, / The sun of my smile, / The ride of my breasts, / The grace of my style.' "

Hold it. Did she say *breasts*? Isn't that illegal in speech?

No way. I had to get out of there.

" 'I'm a woman / Phenomenally. . . .' "

I bolted so fast, I didn't hear her finish the rhyme.

* * *

Once I was in the hallway, the phenomenal fifteen-year-old woman's tears came. I maturely pretended to have something in my eye, until I left the speechies behind for the far side of the building. Blindly, I followed hallways and staircases as far as they would go, winding up finally at the women's locker room in the basement. I tried the door and went in.

The rows of benches and lockers stood silent. My foot-steps echoed. I found the toilet stalls, locked myself in one, and slouched against the wall.

Janell Kelly, my best friend since we'd moved to Lincolnville, my best friend since forever, my *dama,* man—a traitor. And to think I'd worried about sparing her feelings, nixing the idea of escorts for the court so she wouldn't have to rent one or something. I could ask Clarence, and Leda could still ask Willie, but who could Janell invite? Her French horn?

Well, I didn't need her artsy impression of my life. She could shove that poem, and the party for all I cared.

After a while, I went and washed my face, waiting for the pink in my eyes to fade and feeling sorry for myself. Even though I didn't want Janell anywhere near my *quince* now, I hated to think of replacing her. I knew it wouldn't be easy.

*　　*　　*

As composed as possible, I headed back to the auditorium that was serving as team base. I noticed that Mr. Axelrod had put in a late appearance, and I waved down the row of theater seats, but he was talking to Ms. Joyner and didn't see me, or pretended not to. Leda noticed me, though. In a navy linen jumper and T-shirt, her hair drawn back in a long ponytail, she looked almost puritanical.

"Yo, Paz, what happened to you? Kelly said you walked out of her round. She's really pissed."

"*She's* pissed?" I sniffed. "Leda, she was reading this positively pornographic poem that she picked—*especially* for my *quince*," I said, rolling my eyes.

Leda wasn't disturbed. "How much porno could a poem picker pick, if a poem picker could pick porn?"

"I'm not *kidding*, Lundquist." I threw up my hands. "I don't need this crap! I've gotta go check on my ranks." I spun on my heel and left her there.

Before I could reach the scheduling board, my O.C. teammate came galloping up and threw herself at me in a hug.

"I made finals! I made finals!"

"That's great, Vera," I said when she let me breathe again. A small, dim, twenty-watt bulb of hope switched on inside my brain. "What about . . . me?"

Vera looked at me blankly, then shook her head and mumbled a few names from the roster. "Next time, huh, Violet?"

168

★   ★   ★

After watching Vera's Miss Sippy mow them down in finals, I sat grimly through the awards ceremony next to Leda, with Janell on her other side. Our team took first in five events, including Vera's first win, and placed in several others. This time, Zeno won in both Interp and his duet with Trish. The guy was an acting genius.

Our numbers were good. Even though we didn't have a full team this year, being void in three events, Tri-District earned the team trophy, and Ms. Joyner sent our senior Extemper, F. David Worthington, to the podium to receive the award. F. David, golden from head to jeweled fingers to Italian-loafered toes, was a long, tall, vanilla milk shake of a seventeen-year-old guy, sweet to look at but too rich for my blood. He'd missed the first few tournaments because his family was in Belize.

F. David held the Stanley Cup–sized trophy over his head and war-whooped while somebody snapped a picture. "I just want to thank the judges for giving Tri-Dist this trophy . . . because, basically, we deserve it!"

The team went ballistic with shouts, making the coaches get all serious with us, but you could tell they were pleased. As the tournament broke up, I saw Mr. Soloman congratulate Vera, who was hugging her trophy like an Oscar.

Humph. When Mr. S. gave me my judges' critiques ranking me two and two, I didn't say a word, even though I must have just missed making finals. Some of us could be humble.

However, in a few short hours, it would be Saturday

night. Halloween night. Headless-date night. I was going to go home and transform myself. I had finally put together a costume, something wild, something no one else would be wearing. And "humble" was not how I'd describe it.

24

The Clark basement, decorated to look like a dungeon, oozed with costumed humanity. Indecipherable stereo bass boomed, black and strobe lights cut the gloom, and steam from dry ice hissed from the corners. Zeno, attired in doublet, hose, and plumed cap, with medieval shackles on his wrists, must have been auditioning for the lead of *Hamlet in Chains*. His entourage clustered tightly about him: Trish and her boyfriend, Slade Gale, star quarterback for the already-losing Tri-Dist Tridents, and some other upperclass speechies, including F. David Worthington, and their dates. Zeno's status, as fate would have it, was massively single; he'd broken up with last year's class president when she went away to U. of Illinois in September. Zeno's friends all wore theatrical costume, and the rest of the milling crowd didn't look too shabby either.

Dad had dropped me off alone, since Leda was riding with Janell. I scanned the room from the steps but couldn't pick either of them out in the half-dark, half-strobed-out dankness. I made my entrance solo, in an outfit inspired by Mom's mannequin inventory at the thrift shop—down vest, grass skirt, sombrero, and tights, plus the Frankensteinian capper: green face makeup and a pair of used ski boots. Only now it seemed more gaudy than hilarious. You couldn't miss me. But no one seemed to notice.

Waving hello in Zeno's direction, I lumbered over to the refreshment table and helped myself to a cup of blood-red punch and some of that awful candy corn, just to have something to do. The line of grotesque creatures forming behind me forced me to move aside. I ended up standing by the garbage can, watching people throw out used cups and plates.

Where was Vera? I scanned the room for masked goblins about her height but didn't think she'd be a clown, a trash can with arms and legs, or Yoda. Maybe she wasn't here yet. I hadn't worn a mask myself since the third grade, when I ran into a mailbox because the eyeholes of my Cat Woman mask kept sliding up. I thought I'd hit a car, or a car had hit me, and I started to cry in front of all the trick-or-treaters on my block. That kind of incident will make a person swear off masks for good.

Aha! Here came someone I knew. Enter, a tall somebody wearing a cow mask and dressed from head to toe in

Chicago Bulls wear, from jersey to shorts, leggings, socks, and bright-white shoes with red and black trim. Dark arms stuck out from the tank top, another clue. And who else on the team was that tall, other than F. David (who was probably a chess aficionado, not a basketball fan)? I propelled my booted legs in the bull's direction, then stopped short.

An identical Bullsman stepped out from behind the first one, like some cheap carnival trick, and then another, and another, each as tall, dark, and anonymous as the first. They split up and seeped into the crowd. The Williams brothers, Extempers all. Had to be. But which was which?

Before I could puzzle them out, Leda and Janell arrived. The music stopped just as they descended the basement stairs under the black light, and heads turned. Leda was some sort of Victor/Victoria—a woman impersonating a man impersonating a woman. She'd tucked her hair into a beaded skullcap, stuffed her bra with who-knows-what, and tried to fill out one of her mother's black evening dresses, with a pair of men's trousers sticking out through the skirt slits. For extra effect, she carried the cigar she'd won from Marianao, stuck in a cigarette holder.

As for Janell, she had not put together an ungainly blend of winter and summer clothing and ski boots from the local thrift shop, like someone I knew who wished she'd at least thought about trying to look chic. No, Janell was a black-lit apparition in a body-colored leotard, with slivers of white chiffon scarves that glowed purple sewn on like feathers. They swayed with her movements and made her seem to float above the shadowed floor. A white see-through half mask lent her a sexy air of mystery. Janell looked hot. And I felt a cut of jealousy seeing the unmasked guys eye her costume.

Studiously I turned my sombreroed head away, made for one of the Bullsmen, and struck up an emergency conversation.

"Great party, huh?" I said, looking up into a smiling cow's face, probably as close as he could get to a bull mask.

The cow regarded my ensemble. "What are you supposed to be—the Jolly Green Midget?" His voice was much more nasal than Clarence's, but that could've just been from the mask.

"I'm Frankenstein on vacation," I answered, indignant.

"Oh."

"I like your costume," I complimented him, "but someone else had the same idea, I see. Heh-heh."

A bovine pause.

"Look," said the cow, "do I know you? Are you a senior?"

"I don't know, I mean, no. I'm a sophomore. And I don't know if I know you. I mean, who are you?"

An impatient bovine pause. "I'm the Chicago Bull, what does it look like? Hey, I've got someone . . . I've gotta go."

Certain that the blood-red glow from beneath my green makeup was outglaring the strobe light, I turned and sidled away, as well as one can sidle in ski boots.

"Hey, Violet, how ya doing?" Gina from gym class greeted me. She was dressed as a skeleton. Under the black light, the white bones painted on her dark tunic and the permanent morbid smile crayoned onto her face flashed a chalky purple.

I gulped some oxygen. "Wow, Gina, you look really cool."

"Thanks. Where'd you get that costume?"

"Oh, heh-heh, I made it myself. Could you tell?"

"Uh, yeah. What's it s'posed to be?"

"Frankenstein on vacation," I said, thinking this question was going to get old fast.

She smiled. "That's pretty good. You're in O.C., right? That must be fun."

"Yeah, it's great. Like being in a comedy club. What about you, Dramatic Interp?"

"That's right. Me and Zeno Clark. I might as well be acting in a broom closet for all the attention I'm getting."

"Ha, I know what you mean."

She looked at me oddly, as though I couldn't possibly know what she meant, but I *was* wearing a grass skirt and ski vest. Maybe that was it.

"Well," said Gina, "where's the food around here? Let's get some punch."

I made a nontactful point of not speaking to Janell, who was standing around with her Verse teammate, as I went past. I followed Gina to the table and got another cup of punch, but when I turned, Gina was gone.

The stereo boomed, and ghouls swirled around me. I picked out Leda in her he-she costume, chatting it up with two Chicago Bulls who sat on a sheet-draped sofa along one wall. Maybe she had figured out which one was Clarence. I started over, then jerked to a stop. These boots weighted me to the floor when I wanted them to, that was for sure. I stood there, leaden.

Leda had climbed onto the lap of one of the Bullsmen and slung an arm around his shoulders. They all laughed as Leda stuck her cigar in his mouth, where it lodged in the mask. She tried pulling on it, but the Bull finally had to take his mask off to loosen the stogie and get it out of there. The strobe light cut their movements to shards, and the blasts of bass enhanced their waves of laughter.

When the Bull finally tugged his mask off, I stared grimly.

It was Clarence.

25

Mom picked me up. "Isn't it a little early?" she asked. "I wasn't expecting your call so soon. It's not even the witching hour yet."

I didn't say anything. I thought I might explode.

Our house was silent as a tomb when we returned. Dad, still on the early shift, was already in bed; Mark was off at a friend's watching scary movies. Feeling like the undead myself, I unsnapped my ski boots at the door.

Mom scurried into the kitchen and plopped down at the table, where her notebook lay open. I must have called her away from her doodling.

"More restaurant ideas?" I asked. "Lay 'em on me."

"Hmmm? Oh, I'm just looking over the community college catalog, making some notes."

Due to my mood, I didn't recognize this as the giant red flag that it was.

I tossed my sombrero on the Death Throne in the corner and got the milk and chocolate syrup from the fridge to make hot chocolate. I needed some comfort food.

Mom looked up from her work. She knew my life had just fallen apart in some unexplained manner, but she didn't press me about it. "Why don't you let me finish the hot chocolate for you, Vi, hon? Go on upstairs and change. There's a surprise from your grandmother on your bed."

With my boots off, I flew upstairs to my bedroom and shut the door. Having waited for this moment all day, I was ready to cry in the privacy of my own room. A few sobs rose, only to be swallowed when I saw Abuela's gift on my pillow. Quickly I stepped out of my grass skirt and peeled off my tights, slipped into a pair of sweatpants, and went to investigate.

On my powder-blue pillowcase perched a jeweled tiara, like the ones I'd scoffed at in my *quince* book. But this wasn't some Miss America–type rhinestone crown. This headpiece was elegantly simple, a hammered silver ring beaded with tiny freshwater pearls, silvery pink nuggets that looked good enough to eat. And though the metal was highly polished, the piece looked old—antique. It must have belonged to Abuela. Given to her, maybe, by her grandmother. The small card next to it read, TO VIOLETA IN

HONOR OF YOUR FIFTEEN YEARS. LOVE, ABUELA. Reverently, I reached for the tiara and placed it on my head.

As I turned to catch my reflection in the round mirror over my dresser, I started. Frankenstein meets Tiffany's! That would have been a better costume, I thought wryly. I ran downstairs to show Mom, just as the doorbell rang.

"Can you get that?" Mom called from the kitchen. "The candy is in the bowl on the floor."

I grabbed the bowl and answered the door.

"Trick or treat!" came the unison threat.

The visitors stared at my alien princess getup, and I gaped back at them.

There, on the porch, dressed as both man and woman, stood Leda Lundquist. And beside her, Janell.

★   ★   ★

My *damas* wrestled me upstairs and into my room without further ado. Janell, strong as a kick-boxing ox, pulled one arm; Leda, bony knuckles indenting my other wrist, pushed. It felt like I was being hustled by the Mob to a waiting black sedan. The *quinceañero* book hadn't said anything about possible abuse of power by *damas*.

"Why don't you guys just leave me alone?" I whined as Janell sat me forcefully down at my desk.

"Oh," said Leda, shutting the door. "So you can just, like, not deal with us?"

"You guys are being real jerks!"

"Oh, shut up, Violet. You sound like my dad, blaming everybody else." Janell took a seat on my bed and looked me in the eye through her half mask. "You're being the idiot, and you are going to talk to us and tell us what we want to know. Then, if you want, we'll leave."

Leda wordlessly reinforced the threat, her back to the closed door.

I couldn't believe this. After all the incredible crap today, my two ex-best friends—neither of whom I wanted to see at this particular juncture—were ganging up on me. In the last twelve hours I had lost a tournament, a maybe-possible boyfriend, and two best friends, who were about to add insult to injury. If I couldn't count on them now, how could I count on them at my *quince?* Janell looked back at me, mouth stiff beneath her mask, waiting for an answer.

Leda guarded the door fiercely, eyebrows raised. "*Well?*" she challenged.

The sinking sadness in me went sour. Hmph. I didn't have to answer to her—a fourteen-year-old, for one thing. And Janell . . .

I was about to give Janell a piece of my mind when I caught my reflection in the mirror again. My eyebrows clenched low, my lips punched up. Finger streaks marred my green Frankenstein makeup, and Abuela's tiara sat roughly askew.

I looked ridiculous.

My shoulders started to shake. I squeezed my eyes shut, but the shakes still came. Then the tears, as I opened my eyes, and then the laughter.

The girls looked bewildered.

"Hey, are you crying?" asked Leda, coming closer.

"Or what? What's the matter?" asked Janell with concern.

I was laughing too hard now to explain. I pointed at the mirror, my tiara.

They eyed each other, then me. And joined in.

When she could speak, Janell pointed at me and gasped, "Wh-what're you? Princess Leia with a hangover?"

"*HA!*" Leda shouted, followed by three rumbling shakes. Mom's laugh was contagious.

"Did I hear somebody crack a joke?" The door opened and Mom walked in with a tray of steaming mugs. "Hot chocolate, anyone?"

We calmed down enough to take the drinks from her, giggles spurting on and off like an artery had opened. Mom left us alone, and I got up and went to my closet for a T-shirt.

"I'm boiling in this down vest," I admitted. My green makeup had run from the sweat and tears, and I got some on my shirt in the switch, but what the hell. I righted my tiara and sat back down with my hot chocolate, next to my friends.

"Look, Violet," Janell said. She had taken off her mask. "What happened to you today in my Verse round?"

I thought back to this afternoon and writhed. "Er, it was—that poem."

"The Maya Angelou?"

"Yeah, the woman thing."

Janell waited, but an answer was not forthcoming.

"And your problem would be . . ."

"It was too racy," I blurted out.

"Racy?"

"Well, there were, like, body parts discussed." I suddenly knew how Mark felt on the subject.

"She means sex was implied," translated Leda.

"Well, for God's sake, Violet!" Janell tossed up her hands, exasperated. "Doesn't that go with the whole 'woman' thing?"

I couldn't deny that.

"Yeah, Paz, maybe it's your outlook that needs some work," Leda added.

"Hey, it's my outlook and I'll stick with it. It's just—I can't help it, I'm embarrassed talking about that stuff. Or possibly standing onstage while someone else talks about it."

"Maybe you just need to understand the poem better," Janell suggested. "You didn't even hear the whole thing."

She was right. I could at least be fair.

"Okay," I said. "Do it."

★　★　★

Janell *was* right. The poem was perfect. Even though it was a little . . . candid.

The part at the beginning, where the poet says she's not a fashion model; that's true of most women. And later on, she tells about these men who go nuts over her "mystical" charms—they're really going nuts over her, as a woman, just as she is. No mystery.

Janell reached the last stanza. " 'Now you understand / Just why my head's not bowed. / I don't shout or jump about / Or have to talk real loud. / When you see me passing, / It ought to make you proud.' "

I smiled, flashing on Dad.

" 'I say, / It's in the click of my heels, / The bend of my

hair, / The palm of my hand, / The need for my care. / 'Cause I'm a woman / Phenomenally.' "

" 'Phenomenal woman, / That's me,' " we finished together.

"Awesome," said Leda. "A feminist slant is exactly what this ritual needs."

"It already has one," I pointed out. "Remember? We threw tradition in the toilet and flushed hard."

Janell hung an arm around me. "It's going to be a great party," she said, so sincerely that it brought a guilty taste to my mouth; I had been intent on replacing her as *dama* only a short while ago.

"There's still one thing I've got to tell you, Abominable Woman," I said, addressing Leda.

She took her cigar out of the breast pocket of her jacket and wiggled it at me, Groucho Marx–style. "Say the secret woid."

"Stop messing with my man," I said, snatching Leda's cigar and thrusting the thing into my trash can.

"Hey!"

"Thank God," Janell said. "That cigar has seen better days."

"Aw, come on," Leda protested. "All right, I'm sorry. I got a little carried away at the party, but I was not making a move of any sort on your man. I didn't even know Clarence *was* your man."

"Neither does he," I confessed. "But tonight was supposed to be the night."

"Then how come you weren't over there, camping out on his lap?"

"I didn't know who he was until he took off that mask!"

"What a messed-up night," Janell said, finishing her hot chocolate.

Leda nodded. "I second the motion."

We sat there for a minute.

"I don't know," I said, offering an apologetic smile. "It didn't end up so bad."

26

The next day, I phoned my aunt Luz in Portland.

"Hi, Tía? It's me."

"Hey, Violet, *¿qué te pasa?* I haven't heard from you in ages. I was just getting ready to call you."

Tía Luci always makes me feel that way—like she's just been thinking about me and I've read her mind. It occurred to me that Señora Flora had given me that same impression.

"How're you doing, Tía? I miss you."

"Good, kiddo. What's up?"

"Oh, brother. You won't believe the Halloween I had."

"No me digas."

I did say. I told her all of it, and how I'd almost lost both my *damas de honor* in one night.

"Oh, that's bad," Tía commiserated. "I knew a girl when I was growing up who lost her entire court to the German measles."

"Well, I do have one problem. That's why I'm calling."

"Aha."

"Señora Flora is having trouble finding a band that can play both 'Guantanamera' and 'Sweet Home Chicago.'"

Tía Luci chuckled. "No blues *salseros* in your neighborhood?"

"Huh-uh. Do you have any ideas?"

"Sure. I'll do the music."

"You're in a band?"

"No, I'll DJ it. I used to have a radio show in college. I've got some smokin' tapes."

"Hey, that sounds great, Tía. Really?"

"It'll be my gift to you," she said. "I'll start working on some new mixes right away."

"Cool. And . . . another thing."

"Shoot."

"I've got this semester project coming up for Spanish, and Leda and me are doing it on Cuban music. But Dad gave us these really old-fashioned tapes that don't have anything to do with today. We were wondering if maybe you know of some newer music? Something we can relate to?" Leda had begged me to ask. We'd checked the Web, but there were so many sites, we didn't know where to start. And we were still waiting for books from the library.

"*¿Qué? Chica,* you mean you haven't heard of ¡Cubanismo!? Muñecas de Matanzas? Los Van Van?"

I had to say no.

"Ay, ay, ay," she said, sorry for me. "I'll FedEx you some tapes tomorrow."

"Plus we need some info. And maybe the lyrics. We have to be able to write a report on this."

A silence as she realized Dad was of no help. "I can jot down some notes, give you some references. So, you asked Alberto?"

"Dad said he only listened to rock and roll growing up. Didn't you like the same stuff?"

"Oh, believe me, I did. But I grew up with Papi's old records from the Golden Age too."

"Dad said he was embarrassed by them."

Luz sighed. "I guess I was lucky; I was still a little girl when we moved to Chicago from Miami. I was just one of the *muchachas.* Alberto was in junior high, though, and it wasn't easy being the boy from Little Havana. The way some of the kids treated him, like he just got off the banana boat . . . I saw what that did to him. It was like he wanted to prove he was all apple pie."

"So? What's to stop him from listening to the new stuff now?"

She clucked her tongue. "You couldn't even buy Cuban pop music in this country until a couple of years ago, thanks to the embargo. I found that out when I started going to Cuba rallies and listening to the Latino hour on public radio. . . . I felt like I'd been missing something.

That music was in me. I just had to catch up." She puffed a laugh. "So maybe Alberto will too, someday!"

"Maybe. I think what Dad needs is to make his *quince*," I joked.

"Claro que sí," said Tía.

★　★　★

Monday morning I found a note taped to my locker: HERE'S MY NUMBER. CALL ME. CLARENCE.

Why didn't he just call *me*?

Probably because I was so gracious and witty the last time. I always kept them coming back for more. Still, he gave me his number.

Hoo boy. Now I had to call him. I carried the note around all day, arguing with myself that maybe a correspondence relationship might be enough.

Leda caught me rereading the note for the trillionth time on the bus home.

"What's that?"

I refolded the tired creases. "Oh, nothing, really. Just a guy's phone number . . ."

She snatched it away from me with an animal squeal. "You're gonna call him." She said this like it was a true fact already.

"Well, I don't know, I—maybe I should wait for him to call me?"

She thrust Clarence's note back in my face. "You are going to call him." She said this like a threat.

"Okay, okay. I'll call him when I get home."

★　★　★

I scouted the house: Mom was still at the thrift store, Dad would be home pretty soon. Mark had let himself in after school and was in the backyard doing something absorbing with a shovel. I didn't want to know.

I found Chucho asleep under the piano bench and brought him to the kitchen phone with me for moral support.

"Clarence?" I said when a male voice answered.

"Wait, I'll get him."

How many brothers did he have?

He answered. "Hello?"

"Hi, Clarence, it's Violet." I petted Chucho to stay calm; petting dogs is supposed to lower your blood pressure.

"God, Violet, hi! I wasn't sure you'd call."

That made two of us. "Well, you know, I might have won that publishers sweepstakes, or something."

He laughed. "You could be a winner! No, sorry, not today. I just wanted to say I missed you the other night at the party."

How could anyone have missed me? "You didn't recognize me either?"

"I did, I was just waiting till the costume judging for the unmasking. Didn't want to spoil the surprise."

I recalled the identical Bullsmen. "Your brothers! How many brothers do you have, anyway?"

"There are seven of us. Thomas is married, Jasper's in med school, Silas is stationed in Saudi, Dale works at O'Hare, Herbert and Richard are in community college, and I'm the youngest. Or shall we say, the freshest?"

"Well, I met one of your brothers at the party. Who won the costume contest, anyway?"

"Slade and Trish for Bonnie and Clyde."

"Lame."

"Yeah," he agreed. "Well, look, Violet, I hope you're not mad or anything."

"Hey, it was a masquerade party," I said, shrugging off the incident. He hadn't given Leda his phone number.

"Good. I was hoping you might want to go out sometime?"

I realized I was petting Chucho with a vengeance; he squirmed and jumped off my lap.

"Sure," I said.

"Great, I'll let you know."

I hung up, wondering, Did he just ask me on a date? But he hadn't invited me anywhere; he'd asked for a rain check.

Great, I'll let you know. They were the most romantic words anyone had ever said to me.

★　★　★

So I forgot all about Tía Luci's package, and sure enough, on Wednesday, right after my piano lesson, here came the deliverywoman. Funny, you always hope it's for you when you see the truck parked on your street, but it never is. Now the one time I was actually expecting a special delivery, it slipped my mind, and I wasted all that good anticipation.

I accepted the envelope and opened it: two tapes and a bunch of photocopied notes and newspaper articles. And instructions from Tía:

1. Read the stuff about Cuban music first. NO cheating!
2. Play the tapes Alberto gave you and see if you didn't learn something.
3. Play the new tapes—& dance!

I showed Dad, who had just walked in the kitchen door wearing his white pharmacist's uniform over a pair of plaid slacks, with brown rubber-soled work shoes. Weariness tinted his usually animated face. The schedule had been getting the best of him lately. But he brightened a little on reading Tía's note.

"Veo la luz," he said, as he does when his sister, Luz, impresses him. *I see the light.* "She's laid out the whole music history here," he marveled, leafing through the assembled literature. "Can I have a look at it when you're through?"

I nodded. "It's fantastic. The project'll practically write itself. So we won't be needing your help after all, Dad." I expected to see his eyes shine with relief, but disappointment filled them instead. "Until the end," I added. "Would you read the final draft of our report?"

This mollified him, and he even whistled "Cielito Lindo" on his way upstairs.

I called Leda to come over, and we took turns reading to each other in my room. We followed Tía Luci's directions explicitly, even the dancing. After all, no one was around. And what if Luz *could* read my mind?

"This stuff rocks," Leda summed up when we got to the new music. "But they couldn't have done it without the old rhythms."

"What's weird is how they banned Cuban music here along with everything else under the embargo. Tía told me you couldn't buy these tapes until recently." I pointed to one of the photocopies. "Because of this 'trading with the enemy' law."

"Hey, that would be a great title for the project: 'Jamming with the Enemy.' "

"Very *creativo*," I said, nodding. "Let's get started."

"Are you kidding?" Leda said, pushing aside Tía's notes. "That's enough to show Señora Doble-U. We've got a whole month to go, dude. Let's wait till the last minute."

27

The month slipped away, as holiday months do. Bam, it was Thanksgiving weekend. Bam, we were back in school. Triple bam: Señora Wong's semester projects were due. And Clarence hadn't asked me out yet. I could've asked him, but then I still would never have been invited on a date. I just wanted that experience; then, I swore to myself, I'd ask guys out whenever I felt like it.

Leda and I turned in our paper and were assigned a presentation slot toward the end of the pack. Our audience would be good and bored by that time. Perfect.

Even the vigilant *señora* was having trouble staying awake by the time our turn came. It had been a week filled with piñatas, tacos, and castanets. We were all about fiestaed out. But the party was just getting started.

Señora Wong called our names, and Leda and I waited a rehearsed beat. And another, until our *profesora* started to glower. Then, as one, we rose.

"What you just heard," I said, "was not the sound of silence."

"What you just heard," Leda picked up, "was the sound of contemporary Cuban music being imported into the United States. Because until recently, recordings by Cuban artists were banned in this country, causing a cultural divide."

"Our presentation will help bridge that divide," I said, with a wave of feeling as I realized this was true.

"Welcome to the world of Cuban music," said Leda.

I popped a tape into the machine and faded in on a searing rhumba. A smile played over Señora Wong's lips.

★   ★   ★

Let's just say, if there had been a final round, we would've been in it. Leda punched me several times afterward, her equivalent of *muy bien,* and suggested I try out for Oratory next speech season.

But it was this season that was giving me trouble. Over the next few tournaments, my O.C. rounds improved, but not consistently. I would beat "Mary Ann Pimpleberry," even Vera in one round, only to collapse in the next. Mr. Soloman promised my ranks would even out. "Practice like crazy," he said. So I did, in my mirror at home, on the bus to tourneys, even on Wednesdays after piano.

With one tournament left before the next onrushing

holiday, I thought I was making progress toward nailing the speech every time. I vowed to put everything else aside and concentrate solely on speech. Vera and I had just arranged for an extra afternoon of work when Mom dropped her bombshell.

We were eating dinner, Mom, Mark, and me—Dad was on swing shift. Mom had made lasagna and garlic bread, and I had fixed the salad.

"So I'll be staying after school on Thursdays, too," I said. Seeing Mom's eyes widen, I added, "Just until speech season ends."

"Well, I have a new schedule to announce, myself."

Mark and I both looked at her.

"I have decided to start school in January. I told your father this morning."

Even if our mouths hadn't been full, we wouldn't have been able to speak.

"I've decided to take some business classes, and you two are going to have some new responsibilities."

That last familiar reference was eclipsed by the mention of business classes. Mom's dream, dead? She must have woken up and smelled the *café,* realized she would never get rich in the restaurant world, even with a whole chain of drive-thru Cuban-Polish bakeries. She would now opt for a prestigious and lucrative, but uninspiring, CEO position over her passion for cooking and organizing. I nearly wept, but I had garlic bread in my mouth.

I swallowed. "Mom," I whimpered, "what about your restaurant plans? The menus, the funny names, the grand openings?"

Mom narrowed her eyes. "Gone."

Gone?

She smiled. "This will be even better. Drumroll, please."

Mark obliged with palms on the table until she had to tell him to quit.

"Catering," she said finally. "Then I can roll all my ideas into one cookie crust. I was thinking, maybe I could start out catering *quince* parties."

"Catering? But what about the business classes?"

"There's a lot more to catering than just cooking. I'll need to know how to run a business. And I can take some other courses I'm interested in too. So I'm quitting the Rise & Walk and enrolling in community college midterm. I've got to start sometime."

I goggled at her. Mark asked if this meant he'd have to quit PONY league baseball. (It was *December,* for God's sake.) Mom said, "We'll see."

I'd have to keep a tighter schedule as well, meeting Mark after school on certain days. I knew this smacked of the dreaded *R* word that Abuela had predicted would be a part of my *quince* year. But priorities had suddenly changed, and I'd have to do my part. My mother had learned a new word. *Fruition.*

★   ★   ★

The Tuesday before our tourney at Forestfield–Evian High–I showed only a little surprise when Mr. Soloman called me into the speech office and told me I'd be working with the head coach that day.

I dropped my books on the floor in disbelief. *"You've got to be kidding!"*

"I'm serious as a heart attack, Ms. Paz." The Ax had come up behind me. "Now, shall we begin?"

I could feel the brown roots of my blondish hair burn red with embarrassment as I hunched over to retrieve my books. Mr. Soloman abandoned me and went off to work with Vera.

The Ax pulled up his desk chair, all business.

"Your coach tells me you're having trouble with consistency and focus."

Nothing like a little secondhand criticism to buck you right up. "Um, yeah, that sounds about right. My critiques are never the same. I've been scoring 1–6, 2–7, 1–5."

"Mmmm," The Ax ruminated, leaning against the desktop.

I tried to swallow my nervousness.

"Let's see your routine," he commanded, and I performed.

"Mmmm," he said again, afterward.

I stood there, waiting for him to pull his thoughts together. How did Leda stand this scrutiny?

Finally, he motioned for me to sit in the chair next to his desk. "You're losing your narrator," he diagnosed abruptly. "Start over."

"Excuse me?"

"Start over as if you were just memorizing your lines, bar by bar, like a musician. Each time, make your narrator be the melody. Your narrator is what holds the piece together."

He was speaking my language. I nodded. "That's the way I learn a piano piece by heart. First the bass part, then the treble."

He clapped his hands and rubbed them together. "You've got it, Ms. Paz. You obviously don't need my help there. Just practice like crazy, et cetera, et cetera."

His matter-of-fact confidence stunned me for a moment, but I managed to look him in the eye. "Thanks, Mr. Axelrod. Thanks a lot." My gaze involuntarily fell on the desktop, and I stiffened. His wife's laughing face peeked out of the picture frame at us. And the envelope marked LETTERS covered a sheaf of papers.

The Ax reached for the stack and pulled one out, sighing. "Letters of recommendation. Well, it's good to see my students going places."

Oh.

I took this as my cue to leave.

"See you at the tourney, then, Mr. Axelrod. And . . . I'm s-sorry—about going through your stuff and everything."

He eyed me, not unkindly.

"We all have our bad days. Don't mention it, Ms. Paz."

★　★　★

I followed The Ax's prescription, even though Mark kept sticking his head in my bedroom and telling me to shut up when I repeated the same couple of lines over and over. I ignored him, my eyes fixed somewhere above his beady ones; it was a good focus workout. By Friday night, I could've performed my O.C. on a unicycle in the middle of a cattle stampede, with a trick monkey on my back.

"Good luck, Violet," Vera said the next morning as we found our names on the board.

"Back at you," I said.

The high school cafeteria was done up in maroon and blue crepe paper, in honor of Forestfield's home tournament, and Evian bottles sprouted everywhere. The Forestfielders seemed to have a booster club for the speech team; observers filled the rooms. The large audience would have bothered me if not for the last, intense forty-eight hours of work on my focus. An elephant doing the cancan on a bowling ball would not have caused me to bat an eyelash. My mind was a steel trap.

Guy "Pimpleberry" gave me a sneer as I sat down in my first round. But he and Ms. Infomercial conferred worriedly afterward, glancing back at me in the hallway.

After Round Two, "Dr. Speak Easy" introduced himself as George VanderHouten and said I'd been great. I didn't want to say I agreed with him wholeheartedly, so I just murmured, "Thanks. You too."

I hurried to Leda's Oratory round, but the door had been closed, and crashing the party was a no-no.

The hallway was empty. I walked to an unlocked exit and stuck my head outside the building. The winter sky stretched low and full, one long whale of a nimbus. A cold wind whipped sharply, with a wet snap that promised snow or sleet. Let it be snow, I thought, pulling back and letting the door fall shut.

I wandered back to the cafeteria and joined my teammates to wait for the final-round postings. When they went up, I didn't rush over right away. I tried to act like I wasn't even worried.

"Yeah, Violet, I know how you feel," F. David Worthington said, pushing his chair back and kicking his feet up on the table. "When you've made final round so many times, it's hardly even worth checking."

I looked at him, suddenly feeling nauseated, and made a beeline for the posters.

Clarence stopped me en route. He gently grabbed me by the forearms in that double grip of his and smiled. "So you've made your first final round. Congratulations."

I turned to jelly. "I . . . did?"

He tried to hold me steady, but I slipped from his grasp and rushed for the posters to make sure it was true.

Unless there was another V. Paz, I was in. I happened to glance over at the coaches' table and saw Mr. Soloman and The Ax watching me, looking pleased. I pumped a fist at them, grinning like a goon, then checked the clock.

Enough fun and games. It was time to get in character.

28

*M*iss Sippy. Dr. Speak Easy. Ms. Infomercial. Mary Ann Pimpleberry. The curly-haired guy, whose driver's ed skit had improved dramatically. And me. The cream of the north suburban Original Comedy crop gathered to compete before a standing-room-only crowd in Room 248 of Forestfield High School. History would be made here today, ladies and gentlemen. I ate an extra sugar cube for luck.

The judge called me second. "Violet—Pazz?"

Surprise! I was actually able to move and speak. I simply imagined Mark sticking his head in the door to bother me, and nothing could shake my concentration.

My siren opening startled the room. I could feel the electricity.

"The story you are about to hear is true. . . ."

Mr. Axelrod would have been proud of me—for about five seconds. I remembered my lines, all right. But I concentrated on them so hard that I rushed my body comedy. People seemed not to get it. After I'd bombed with the conga-line act—and I do mean *no* laughs, *ningún*—even my closing pantomime with the cell bars felt hokey. Today, Marcel Marceau I was not.

Great physical shtick distinguished each of the other acts: Miss Sippy cocked that hip and waggled her neck; Ms. Infomercial overacted her "And, s-t-r-e-t-c-h!"; even Mary Ann Pimpleberry got some laughs with one of those solo hugs that look like you're making out with yourself. The others gave their characters that third dimension too.

Afterward, teammates who had never spoken to me before came up to offer congratulations anyway. Greg Ibarra, Leda, and Janell joined me in the hall. Janell gave me a huge hug, and Leda punched me in the arm, her highest form of praise.

"Way to go," said Greg, who looked neat in a suit, with his straight, short dark hair freshly cut and silver wire-rimmed glasses polished.

"Thanks. Where's Clarence?" I asked, disappointed. "I thought he'd be with you."

He shook his head. "Extempers do have free will, you know."

Thud. He'd chosen not to come.

"Besides," said Greg, "he didn't want to miss his own final round."

Soar. "We both made it?" I'd forgotten to read the rest of the finals postings.

Janell was smiling. "And me, in Verse. I had to run to get here in time."

I squeezed her hand. "This is so great! Come on, let's go find Mr. S.!"

★　★　★

Forestfield's drama department has a real 250-seat theater. Speechies filtered in for the awards ceremony and sat in school clusters. Both Mr. Soloman and The Ax shook my hand.

"How're we doing for team?" I asked them.

"Excellent," said Mr. Axelrod. "Ten of twelve events went to final, and some doubled up, like Ms. Campbell and yourself."

Mr. Soloman consulted his clipboard. "But New Beverly South and Forestfield are close contenders."

Ugh, if Evian High won their own tournament, we'd never hear the end of it.

"Time to chant," said Leda. *"Nam-myoho-renge-kyo . . ."* She struck a yoga position in her seat. Luckily, she was wearing pants.

Clarence and F. David returned from their Extemp round and sat in front of us. Then Clarence made Greg switch seats with him, ending up by me.

"How'd it go?" I asked. "What was your topic?"

Clarence grimaced. "It was a bear. 'Why China Deserves Most Favored Nation Trading Status.'"

"Why does it?"

"Why doesn't it?" corrected Clarence. "At least, that was my point. I editorialized. I'm probably disqualified."

Leda heard this. "Dude, we could use you in Oratory."

"Save me a place," he answered wryly.

The house lights dimmed, and a local speech coach started the show.

Torture! Fifteen events to get through, each placing four to six winners, and finally, the team standings. Suspense began to build early on, when F. David took the first-place Extemp ribbon and Clarence was at least officially recognized with fifth place. Clarence came back to his seat and reached over, and I suddenly found myself holding hands with a guy in a dark theater.

Check that one off my list.

As the awards droned on, Tri-Dist took first or second in nearly every event. The theater came alive with adrenalized kids jogging to and from the stage. Then I was one of them.

"And for Original Comedy," announced the Forestfield coach, "in sixth place, Violet Paz! Fifth place, Guy Chamberlaine . . ." My ears shut down as I concentrated on climbing the stairs, crossing the stage, and accepting my ribbon with the ghost of Father Leone hovering over me. Success! Packing a suitcase full of smiles, I headed back as Vera came forward for her award. Second! And first had gone to the girl from Forestfield, Ms. Infomercial. The hambone actually took the microphone, liter of Evian in one fist, thanked the judges, and said, "And, s-t-r-e-t-c-h!" Mine wasn't the only groan in the audience.

Janell got fourth place in Verse, and by the time Zeno and Trish took first for their duet, the Tri-Dist speechies were pumped. But Forestfield and New Beverly South had also made a strong showing, with lower ranks, but doubling up in nearly every event.

We were neck and neck and neck.

"And now, the moment you've been waiting for," said the Forestfield coach, taking a swallow from her bottle of Evian. "The team awards."

By this time, my amphibious palm had fused to Clarence's larger, spongelike hand. As each place was announced, we both clutched harder.

"Third place, with sixty points: New Beverly South!"

An extremely giddy girl fell all over herself accepting the trophy. "This is for you, Principal Fernandez!" she said with tears in her eyes.

"Second place . . ."

Janell grabbed my other hand and squeezed it.

"with a new team record of sixty-two incredible points . . ."

I couldn't take the pressure.

"our very own, hardworking, talented team: Forestfield High School!"

Janell and Clarence let go. With inward breaths, we looked at one another. Then a spontaneous cheer rose from the Tri-Dist seats.

"And first place . . . with sixty-three points . . ."

I didn't hear her finish.

"Ms. Paz," came a strong, gruff voice in my ear. "You're on."

Amid the mad applause, I turned to find The Ax nodding at me.

The team trophy?

"Me?"

"Well, go on, go on." He waved me away.

And then I was the one falling all over myself, though *not* over the Forestfield coach, as I gripped the first-place team trophy and said through tears into the microphone, "This is the greatest moment of my life. Thank you to the judges here today, and especially to our coaches, Mr. Axelrod, Mr. Soloman, and Ms. Joyner. I thank you, and Tri-Dist thanks you!"

Roars from our side, and applause all around. It wasn't just good sportsmanship, either—who cares about that? We'd sent Zeno to a double win, killed in duets, and then there was the way Vera and I had practically swept O.C. Speechies may keep poker faces during rounds, but they know when someone deserves to win.

We packed up to leave, and Clarence walked me up the theater ramp. "Well, that's it for this year," he said. "I don't know what you're up to, but I'd like to see you during vacation sometime."

Uh-oh, another vague rendezvous.

"Like, next Friday?" Clarence added. "Night?"

"To do . . . ?"

"A movie!" he said triumphantly. "My mom'll drive."

"Sure, Clarence," I said, as though I accepted dates all the time. "Next Friday. That'd be fun."

We pushed through the double doors with the crowd

and stepped outside to a wintry breeze. Giant flakes swirled through the air, seeming never to light.

The year's first snowfall. It was an omen, a pristine start to a beautiful relationship between Clarence and me. Either ours would be a frigid, stormy affair—or the chemistry between us would be hot enough to melt glaciers, flood rivers, and dry them back up again. I was hoping for the latter.

29

I tried to imagine everything that might happen Friday night, so it wouldn't look as though I was on my first date.

Clarence had apologized about his mom having to drive us, but, hey, he was fourteen. What was he going to do, steal a car? And a license? Anyway, he made up for the chaperone bit by picking a really cool place to go. Not the Lincolnville Dozenplex for a matinee. But an evening trip downtown to Water Tower Place to see the new Jackie Chan movie, plus dessert at the chic café next door. Mrs. Williams planned to shop, not sit between us at the movie.

I figured I was guaranteed at least ninety quiet minutes alone with Clarence, give or take any extra time in the pop-

"Sst!" hissed Dad, nodding at me.

Luz did a double take, from me back to her brother. "Dialogue begins at home, *hermano*," she murmured.

"En esta casa, no hablamos de estas cosas."

"Oh, come on, Alberto! That's Papi talking. Civil discourse is not a sin." She threw her chin in my direction. "And you're not helping by keeping them in the dark."

"Yeah," I seconded boldly. I dried my hands on a dish towel and went and stood next to Luz.

"It's all in the history books for anyone to see," Dad said, tight-lipped. "Castro brought this on himself, by taking, taking. The embargo keeps what we have left out of his hands."

"Do you really think that's the way it works? That *el jefe* is the one to suffer?" Luz asked skeptically. "I'm sure he has plenty to eat and the freedom to go wherever he chooses."

"Well, he is president," Mom put in awkwardly.

Dad didn't say anything.

Luz gave an impatient sigh. "For God's sake, this embargo has gone on too long. More than thirty years! Families have been ripped apart. The rights of the Cuban people have been ignored. The rights of Americans to travel have been trampled on too, by the way. That's all we're saying."

Dad leaned forward. "Oh, so you're a spokesman for this group now?"

"Maybe." She nodded. "I think you'd like what they have to say, if you'd listen. I thought you were all for democracy, *mi hermano*."

"I trust in the government to make the decisions."

Luz pinned eyes on him. " 'We the people,' Alberto. 'We the people.' "

*　*　*

The two black sheep sat on the bed in the guest room, backs against the wall. An uneasy truce rang loudly in the halls. Luz had tripped the invisible wire in the Paz household.

I had to hand it to her; I wouldn't have done it.

"That was something, Tía," I said. "Nobody ever tries to talk sense into Dad."

"If at first you don't succeed, try, try again." She sighed. "Although I don't even try with your grandfather anymore."

"Dad's face scares me when he talks about Cuba."

"Me too, *chica*. And Papi won't even discuss it." She rolled up one of the bed pillows and smooshed it against her tummy. She looked off into space. "You know, sometimes I'm glad I wasn't born there. Other times, I wish I had been with all my might." Her brown eyes met mine. "It's a hard place to be in."

"Sometimes I think Dad just doesn't care."

She hesitated. "Alberto is another story."

I frowned. "I can't see why."

"Life is a lot more black and white to him. Don't forget, he grew up in the thick of things, in Miami. And, somewhere inside, he remembers leaving Cuba. That's why he and Papi are so close. They've had their differences, but now they have their similarities."

I reached for the other pillow and stuck it between me and the wall. "So, about the embargo—Abuelo feels the same as Dad? That the laws punishing Cuba are how things have to be forever? They never mention it. Not in English, anyway."

"Alberto has learned from the master how to hide his feelings, but sometimes the anger slips out. Papi, he has washed his hands of the whole matter. For him and for Mami, the only Cuba is the Cuba of old. They have no future there anymore, or they think they don't."

"But there's always a chance that things could go back to the way they were. Right?"

The odds sounded slim, just saying it.

Luz sighed. "No one knows," she answered. "That's why they call it the future."

We sat in silence for a few moments.

"So, how go the *quince* plans?"

"They *were* going great," I said ruefully. "We've got our routines mostly together—well, Mrs. Lowenstein is helping me with the last part of my piano medley, and then all we'll have to do is practice."

I elbowed my pillow and searched for a more comfortable position. "Tell me about your trip to Spain, Tía. When you were my age."

A glow entered her dark eyes, not unlike Abuela's reminiscent air. "Was the greatest," she pronounced. "Two weeks of freedom!"

"You went by yourself?"

"No way, *chica*. Mami wanted to go, but she couldn't get two weeks off from her job. I went with my best friend, Carlotta, and my cousin Linda and her mom, Tía Elena. Do you know them?"

I shrugged. "Tell me what you did. Was your Spanish good enough?"

She grinned. "It's like another language, Castilian. But we managed." She scrunched down until she was lying flat, with her legs hanging off the bed. "We wandered the streets of Madrid, with Tía Elena, of course. Then we took the train to the countryside and stayed in this huge stone castle. Tía Elena left us alone once we were out of the city."

Yow, alone in an exotic foreign country! I could see why Leda wanted to go. "So what did you do there?"

She laughed. "Looked for cute guys."

"Find any?"

She laughed again. "Oh, yeah. It was the best time I've ever had, to this day." She sobered. "But there was more to the trip than that."

"What do you mean?"

"It was when I got back." She closed her eyes. "I remember Papi came to meet me at O'Hare. When I got off the plane, he was the first person I saw, right up in front, and he was carrying a bouquet of two dozen long-stemmed red roses. *'Para ti, mujercita,'* he told me."

I could see Abuelo, a younger Abuelo—maybe with hair on his head—handing her the flowers.

"He picked up my bag, gave me his arm, and said, 'Now my Luci has seen things I have never seen. *Estás con los adultos.*' "

"What does that mean? You were—what?"

She opened her eyes, smiling softly. "One of the grown-ups."

We sat wrapped in the scene for a minute.

Then a soft knock came on the door, and Mom opened it. "Can I come in?"

We made room, and she sat on the foot of the bed.

"Tía was just telling me about her *quince* trip, Mom."

"To Spain?"

Luz nodded. "And how grown-up Papi made me feel when I got home. I'll never forget that."

Mom looked at the two of us, measuring, discerning what we'd been talking about. "There's lots of Teodoro in Albert, isn't there?"

Tía and I looked at each other. "There sure is," we said together.

*   *   *

Dad, home from the night shift, took Tía and me out for breakfast before her flight the next day. The mood in the house had improved after we girls had talked the night before. Somehow, it had spilled over onto Dad.

"*Pues, mi hermanita,* I'm glad you made it for Christmas," Dad said to Tía. "And thanks for those CDs."

He seemed sad to see her go now and promised to call more often. She teased him all through the meal and promised to call before she showed up next time. It was a running joke of theirs, and it shed some sunshine on the cold, overcast morning outside.

I breathed a sigh of relief, thinking that Mom must have had something to do with the sudden December warmth.

30

The weather got so crazy around New Year's that it kept us inside for several days. Funny how you can be endlessly bored for a while, and then everything happens at once. Vacation ended, and I had a pop quiz in English the day Mom started at community college. This illustrious date was shared with both Mark's birthday and *el día de los tres reyes*, the day when Cubans celebrate the visit of the three wise men, twelve days after the birth of the Christ child.

Abuela and Abuelo and Luz, who was in Miami, called that afternoon to wish us a happy Cuban Christmas and happy birthday to Mark. Then Abuela stayed on the line to say that my invitations had gone out in the mail. She had compiled a guest database and streamlined the whole mailing process by computer, using her e-mail address for RSVPs. I would have other duties.

"Let me talk to your father," Abuela said when she finished with me.

I watched and listened as Dad answered her questions over the phone, using staccato Spanish at first, then fading to a compliant English: "Yes, Mami. No, Mami. I will."

He hung up, looking suitably cowed. Today was also the fateful day of our dance lesson with Señora Flora.

★ ★ ★

Mark gladly went down the block to his buddy's to play new video games for a couple of hours while Dad and I went to keep our dance date. We pulled up to the Arlington Heights party-planning headquarters just as dark was settling in under a low gray sky. More snow coming.

Dad was nervous. "Why couldn't your mother come?" he grumbled, knowing she was at school.

"Dad, how are you supposed to learn to dance if Mom brings me?"

"How am I supposed to–?" he broke off, smiling. "I'm just a slow learner, that's all. We'll give it a try."

I was in the same boat but didn't let on. "I brought some of Tía Luci's tapes too. Just for fun." Maybe Flora would show us some salsa moves.

Fauna received us with deference, and when she turned to summon her sister, I could have sworn she winked at me through her magnifying glasses.

"What did she mean by that, I wonder–*amigos del Papa*?" Dad mused.

"You must be Señor Paz." Flora greeted us with out-stretched hands. Before Dad could change his mind, she led us down a corridor and into a large dance studio with a bare wooden floor and a wall of gleaming mirrors.

"Am I to assume this is a first lesson for you both?"

We nodded. How could she tell? To fit in, Dad had even worn his vintage seventies disco outfit, though he'd never danced in it.

"I can explain . . . ," Dad began.

Señora Flora raised a finger. "Ah, ah. No need. Now, no more talking. Say it with your hips." We watched as she introduced us to the steps for salsa and merengue.

My hand went up. "Is this going to be on the test?" I joked.

"Trust me," she said. "After these steps, the waltz will be a breeze."

She showed Dad how to lead and me how to follow, then turned us loose. Our knees knocked together (well, mine hit his shins) dancing salsa, and our hands got clammy doing the merengue. This was my usual dance experience.

"Let's come back to that," Flora said. "Señor Paz, may I have this *baile*?"

She put a waltz on, heavy with strings and horns that seemed to sweep them across the floor naturally. *One*-two-three, *one*-two-three, *turn*-two-three—and Dad was dancing! After a few circuits, Flora handed him over to me.

She was right, waltzing was a breeze, no syncopation to worry about. Dad seemed more confident too. Our knees still collided every now and then, but gracefully so.

"How am I doing, Violet?" Dad puffed.

"Great!"

After a while, Flora stopped the music. "*Muy bien.* I'll lend you the video, and you'll practice some more at home. Now, let's see those tapes your aunt sent, Violet." She selected a frenetic salsa number by Los Van Van and left us alone in the studio.

I started nodding to the beat. Dad wagged a hip. After all, nobody was around. Our eyes met in the mirror on the far wall, and we exchanged grins. And began to dance.

★ ★ ★

Not one to look a good mood in the horse's mouth, I took the opportunity on the drive home to bring up the class trip to Mexico. Dad's head had been in the clouds ever since Señora Flora had praised his innovative blend of merengue and the macarena at the end of our session.

I interrupted his falsetto vocal interpretation of "Cielito Lindo."

"Dad, can I ask you something?"

"Sure." He smiled in my direction.

"I know it's kind of early, but next fall the junior and senior Spanish classes are going on a trip to Mexico. You know, a cultural thing. I'd only be in second year, but they'd let me go. You'd have to sign a permission slip. And I was wondering if, I wondered, that is . . . if I could go too."

His smile faded.

"If I got a job, I'd have almost a year to save up," I added quickly.

He outright frowned. "Jobs? Trips? These don't sound

like appropriate activities for someone your age, who is only—"

"Who is *only* fifteen," I reminded him, "the same age as Luz was when she went to Spain for her *quince.* And by then I'll be sixteen."

He pursed his lips in silence.

"I'll have to ask your mother" was all he finally said.

★   ★   ★

Weeks went by, and Señora Wong handed out the permission slips for early reservations for next year's trip. They needed an estimate to give to the travel agent.

I took my slip home but didn't bring up the subject again. If Dad didn't want me to go, I wasn't going. I don't think he even talked it over with Mom. Luz was right. Dad seemed to be purposely trying to keep me in the dark, to keep me from breaking the spell that he'd cast, the cocoon he'd spun to shield himself from thinking about Cuba. It would be easier for me to just take German next year with Leda.

Meanwhile, speech season had started up again, and the balance had shifted. Just when I thought I was getting a handle on Original Comedy, I found myself lost in unfamiliar territory. The state schedule had us competing outside our district now. New faces and routines jostled me from my spot in the pecking order. Some to my advantage, to be sure; I was introduced to a whole new round of bad jokes. But other kids were *good.* My Loco Family took a sound trouncing, two tourneys in a row.

So I shouldn't have been surprised when I was cut from the next competition, an overnight trip downstate to the

Middleville tournament. The team roster was posted outside Mr. Axelrod's office, as though we'd gone straight to final-round announcements. Greg, Gina, and a few other speechies hovered there at lunchtime when I went by.

"Man! Sophomores don't have a chance!" complained a guy who did Humorous Interpretation. His duet partner commiserated.

"I beg to differ," countered Greg, who'd earned perfect ranks twice and snagged the Extemp slot over senior F. David Worthington. He blew on his fingernails boastfully. F. David must have been miffed beyond belief, and had reportedly snapped at The Ax, not improving his chances of ever competing again.

My gym buddy, Gina, gazed sadly at the poster listing Zeno Clark as the Dramatic Interp entry. "The coaches said they could only afford to take one kid from each event. Always a bridesmaid, never a bride," she whimpered.

My face mirrored her sentiments. The O.C. choice was Vera, who'd placed her last three times out. I didn't want to admit it, but I could kind of see the coaches' logic. Vera had been working at it a year more than me.

"I'm out too," I said to Gina. "Looks like Vera has juniority over me."

She gave a weak smile at that.

Cherise Belliard had juniority in Verse over Janell, who would also be staying home. Except for Greg, the rest of the competitors were seniors—with the notable exception of a certain fourteen-year-old sophomore, the lone Oratory representative, who believed strongly in gardening versus meat eating. Leda would be on the bus too.

I'd have a whole Saturday off, for a change. Except that I had to stay home with Mark so Mom could hit the restaurant-equipment convention at McCormick Place. Dad was taking a rare morning off to do lunch with a professor friend in Hyde Park, leaving me stuck with the *responsabilidad* of watching Mark until he got back. Burden, really.

"I'm twelve now!" Mark argued when Mom told us.

"Good. Then you're old enough for hard labor," Mom teased. "I want that driveway shoveled by the time your father gets back." This, she meant.

My brother grimaced, no doubt getting his first taste in a long buffet line of responsibility that would make him grow up big and strong. See how he liked it.

I decided to go ahead with my plan anyway. Since we'd been cut from the team for the weekend, I figured Clarence wouldn't be too busy on Saturday. Now that I had to stay home till whenever, I couldn't ask him to go out to the mall with me, my initial bright idea. So I thought I'd see if he wanted to come over. We could play some music or something.

I squared it with Mom, then called Clarence.

He said he'd be there.

★ ★ ★

Clarence was right on time. I invited him into the kitchen, where I was whipping up a pan of brownies. Leda had said chocolate was an aphrodisiac, which I figured couldn't hurt.

When the brownies came out of the oven, I refilled our pop glasses and steered the guy whom, by the second date, I do believe I could call my boyfriend to the screened-in back porch. My lair had been sealed off from the winter weather with quarter-inch-thick Plexiglas storm windows. The old True Value space heater and some carefully selected slow blues on the boom box made the porch almost cozy.

Clarence and I sat together on the rickety couch, drifting along with the music, not talking much. We were listening to a CD he'd brought over when the sliding door opened and Mark burst through, followed by Dad with an unlit cigar in his hand. Dad wore his favorite yellow shirt with the monkeys on it—he'd gone out in public in that. Mark's face was a chilly pink from shoveling snow.

Dad switched on the ceiling fan and lit up. "Hey, you two. I'm back. Up for some *domino*?" he asked disingenuously, as though I hadn't spent fifteen minutes the night before telling him when and where *not* to let Mark bother me. I'd forgotten to include Dad in that.

"I'm afraid I don't know how to play," Clarence said, removing his warm arm from my shoulder.

"*Es facil,* we'll teach you," Dad insisted, dragging over the card table and setting the domino board on top. He pulled a cassette from the pocket of his monkey shirt and motioned for Clarence to switch the music.

Mark thrust an open palm in my face. "Dad gave me a whole five bucks in dimes!" An overt bribe.

Knowing when I was beat, I cashed in a dollar from my pants pocket and split my dimes with Clarence.

Dad turned the red and white dominoes out of their wooden box onto the board, and we all joined in the shuffling, then chose pieces.

"The biggest double starts. Double nine!" called Dad, to no response. "Double eight!"

"Four, six, eight. That's me!" said Clarence.

And we were off and running.

We had eaten half the brownies and Mark was sitting on a pile of dimes by the time Mom walked in at about six o'clock, with Chucho at her heels. I introduced Clarence to her and Chucho. The dog had been at the groomer's and resembled a genetically modified sheep.

"Clarence," Mom said, still in her coat and boots and carrying a shopping bag of convention freebies. "Nice to see you, but your father has been waiting for you out front in the cold. Didn't anyone hear the doorbell?"

We turned down the Etta James tape and admitted that we hadn't heard a thing. Dominoes will do that to you.

I enjoyed a wisp of a kiss as Clarence hurried out the front door with a few brownies for the road. Mr. Williams waved from the car, and they were gone down the plowed street.

31

The next afternoon, the telephone rang. I got up from practicing my scales on the piano and answered it. Anything to put off scales.

"Hello, Violet?"

That liquid velvet voice again.

"Hi, Clarence. Let me switch phones." I grabbed the cordless and brought it up to my room. "What's up?"

"I just wanted to tell you I had a good time yesterday."

"At my house?"

"Sure." He chuckled softly. "Learning dominoes and everything. It reminded me of your speech. I could really see where some of it came from."

"Yeah, I can't make stuff up."

"Not at all," he argued. "You . . . bring it to life. It's not an easy thing to make others see what you see."

"Really?" This was a skill?

"I wish I could do that."

"I'll bet you can," I said. "Maybe Extemporaneous Speaking isn't right for you. Maybe you *should* be doing Oratory with Leda." He hadn't seen a final round in a while either.

"Hmmm," he murmured into my ear. "I could give it a try. But you, Violet. You've definitely found your event."

"Guess I can't help it if my family is crazy enough to make everyone laugh."

"Yeah! Like when your dad knocked that domino off Mark's head with Chucho's slobbery ball."

I smiled. "Maybe I'll work that into the routine."

"And when he got up and did the macarena–what was he talking about, calling that 'your' dance?"

Now I blushed. And him not here to see my rosy cheeks. "Oh, he was talking about my big *quince* party, coming up in May."

"Your what?"

"*Quinceañero*. It's this Cuban celebration for–being fifteen." I wasn't about to mention the woman part.

"Yeah? Tell me more."

I drew a breath. It's just Clarence, I thought.

I described "All the World's a Stage" and told him how Abuela had come up with the idea in the first place, and how Señora Flora was putting together the party. "But I designed the program."

"And you'll be the star. That sounds perfect for you," he said. "And then there'll be Cuban food and dancing?"

"As Cuban as it gets."

"Interesting."

We paused, and it wasn't uncomfortable.

"I noticed your dad kept calling you Violeta."

A slight embarrassment washed over me, and I remembered what Dad had said about wanting to be American. "He calls me that sometimes."

Clarence cleared his throat. "Violeta. Sounds . . . mysterious. Can I call you that too?"

Jeez, I liked this guy.

"Sure, Clarence."

★ ★ ★

Life took on a new rhythm, for some of us, at least. Clarence came over to play dominoes on days when I had to watch Mark. He was getting pretty good. Mom was busier and busier with classes. Even Chucho displayed a renewed vigor with the coming of the longer days.

But Dad was still stuck in his rut, just working, working, working, or trying to recuperate from work. He and Mom would go out and bowl a few frames or hit some balls at the driving range, but that was about all he could handle. They'd had to give up their leagues.

"Forget about it, *muchacha*," Dad said when I asked him if we could drive out to St. Ignacio's for Mass one Sunday.

"Aw, come on, wouldn't you like to see your friends for a change?"

He sighed wearily. "*Claro que sí.* But I will see them in a couple months, at your *quince.*"

And that was the end of it.

★　★　★

Springtime was slow to arrive. It had been the winter that wouldn't quit, with all the trademarks: power failures, school closings, and snow on Easter. Leda and I had skied a few trips, once at Little Switzerland and twice at giant Alpine Valley. I kind of hated to see winter end.

The speech season had, unfortunately, closed with less of a bang than The Ax would have liked: Tri-Dist took third in state, and Zeno won again, but his and Trish's duet didn't make it out of sectionals, and they had been our stars. The highlight for Janell and me, and a few more kids, was getting back on the roster in time for the second overnighter, the Peekasau tournament. We decorated our motel room with socks and took a picture. This finally shut up Leda's squawking. She had returned from Middleville with a fourth-place trophy . . . and the DO NOT DISTURB/*NO MOLESTE POR FAVOR* sign from her room, which she had taped onto her Spanish folder.

With speech competition over, Leda was back to her old grudging-activist schedule. And I was fielding invitations again.

"Come on, Paz, what could be better than a *raffle*? In *Spanish*?"

Another fund-raiser for the Cuba Caravan. Beth and Niles were dragging her along.

230

"Why don't you ask Janell?"

"She can't make it. Look, you could even bring Clarence–that is, if I can find a suitable date of the male persuasion. You should get him to take Spanish with you next year," she encouraged me. "Then you could travel together on that class trip to Mexico. It could be your honeymoon."

I flushed. "Get out. Anyway, the trip is for juniors and seniors."

I had recently broken the news to Leda that I wouldn't be taking first-year German with her next term. All that new vocabulary was too confusing. Besides, after hearing about Luz's *quince* trip, I really wanted to find a way to go to Guadalajara. Maybe Mexico wasn't as cool as Spain, but it had once been a colony of Spain, or something. And as far as I knew, the school district wasn't sending anyone to Cuba.

"*Please,* Paz, come with me to the rally."

This time I didn't immediately say no. I got up from the purple-covered futon in Leda's bedroom and joined her at the computer. She had asked me over to invite me, in person, to the Cuba rally. And to get me to help her with her Spanish paper, one of those who-do-you-admire things, *en español.* I was writing about Luz.

"I thought I'd do mine on Che Guevara," Leda had said on the phone.

"You admire him?" I asked. I didn't remember her ever mentioning Che.

"No, I just think he has a cool name. Let's get on the Internet and see what we can locate."

As we typed into the search engine, I found myself half-looking over my shoulder for Dad, as though researching Cuba on the Net were right up there with bogus psychics and kiddie porn.

We did some checking and learned that Che Guevara, a partner of Fidel Castro's, helped lead the Cuban peasants out of oppression by the corrupt Batista regime in the 1959 revolution. Che died in Bolivia a few years later, trying to do the same type of thing there.

"He wasn't even Cuban!" said Leda. "I thought he was a big national."

"He was born in Argentina," I read. "It was the cause, not the country, for him." Thinking about this, I could kind of understand Leda's parental units, Beth and Niles, and the Causes. It must feel good trying to do the right thing.

Leda, looking for more background, had punched in *Cuba* and eventually ended up with a list of Cuba-focused peace organizations. I was fascinated. People all over the globe were working to normalize relations with the island. People who weren't even Cuban. I wanted to ask them why.

"That's the one!" Leda said, highlighting a selection with her mouse. "That's the Illinois group that's doing the fund-raiser." She clicked on their site. "There's the notice," she said.

Over the speakers came Latin dance music. The screen read:

PEACE WITH CUBA Rally and Fund-raiser,
2 p.m. Saturday, Aurora Center.

Sponsored by Clergy for Cuba.

Join PWC for an exciting afternoon of Cuban cuisine and music

to raise money for medical supplies.

See video footage of the latest carpentry campaign in Matanzas.

Salsa dance at 5. Book sale and CD raffle!

Jeez, a raffle. What could be better than that?
The Lundquists would be there. Maybe I would too.

32

*O*ver the next few days, the different faces I'd seen on the Cuba Web sites haunted me. Questions I couldn't ask at home bubbled up relentlessly in my mind, only to pop unanswered. So, on Saturday, I went with Leda to the Cuba thing.

I crossed my fingers and told my folks it was a Free Tibet fund-raiser, figuring what they didn't *sabe* couldn't *molesta* them. Mom said, "It's nice of the Lundquists to invite you," and Dad proceeded to warn me of the dangers of peace marches, but said okay when he found out we wouldn't be marching.

The rally was held in the big gym at a community center. Even though Leda didn't have a date, she let me bring

Clarence. I'm sure he earned her some bucks in the walk-about fund. Beth and Niles rushed off to talk to their activist friends, leaving the rest of us to ramble.

Leda, Clarence, and I browsed the book table, picking up some free literature and bookmarks. There was even a printed timeline of U.S.–Cuba events, from the revolution to the missile crisis to the embargo, and beyond. Just what I needed. The people at the table acted normal and nice, not like scheming Communists. They said if I had any questions after I read the pamphlets to e-mail them.

"Check it out, Paz!" Leda pointed to a Che Guevara poster for sale. "I've got to have it."

I was more interested in a coffee-table book about Havana. The streets were alive with people in every photograph. The stone and stucco buildings showed layers of white or pastel paint. Even in a crumbling state, arched doorways and wrought-iron balconies cut magnificent shapes out of a blue sky.

Clarence hung over my shoulder. "Kind of reminds me of New Orleans," he said, pronouncing it "N'awlins." "We have cousins there."

I turned the page to a shot of the Morro Castle, an imposing offshore battlement out in blue, blue Havana Bay.

"What about you, Violet?" Clarence rubbed my neck with his fingers. "Violeta," he said more intimately. "Do you have family in Cuba?"

"No, I . . ." Wait. I always just assumed. "I'm not sure. Maybe."

"That'd be cool," he said.

"Yeah, it would."

We ate mounds of black beans and rice, and squares of *flan* for dessert. I plunked down five dollars for the raffle but didn't win. After some of the organizers from Peace with Cuba spoke and played a video, the dance began.

The three of us stood around in the corner for a while, swaying to the music. When neither Leda nor I made a move to dance, Clarence looked at me and stuck out a palm. "Well?"

I hesitated.

"What are you waiting for?"

Just then, a dark-haired guy wearing two gold earrings and a POWER TO THE PEOPLE T-shirt walked over and touched Leda on the elbow. She ducked her head, leaning closer to hear what he was saying, and then followed him onto the dance floor.

"Er, I'm not waiting for anything," I told Clarence. "Come on. Let's *baile*. Mmmm, merengue, my favorite."

★ ★ ★

Something Clarence had said got me thinking.

"Dad," I asked one evening after he'd worked the day shift. He and Mark were putting together a 3-D puzzle at the kitchen table. "Do we have relatives in Cuba still?"

Mark glanced up.

Dad's face started to harden. I reached out and touched a hand to his arm. "Dad?"

He tensed.

Now both Mark and I looked at him, questioning.

He took a breath. "*Seguro,* many of Mami and Papi's *familiares* continue to live there."

"Do you ever hear from them?" I asked.

His eyes cloaked. "I was just a baby when we left Cuba. I don't remember them. We've sort of–lost contact."

"Do you think I'll ever get to meet them?" asked Mark.

Dad was touched by the question. But he dropped his head to search for another puzzle piece.

"No one knows, little brother," I answered. "That's why they call it the future."

★   ★   ★

Mom was working on restaurant plans again, only this time it was for her final business class project. The catering idea was taking shape.

She and I walked the aisles at Food Depot, Mom jotting down prices for black beans and olive oil, spices and rice. She had to present a bid and then meet her budget.

We paused at the ice cream display.

"Just think, if your *quince* were a few months later, I'd be catering it," she marveled, scribbling something with a nifty mechanical pencil she'd bought. I guess she figured it was time to get serious about office equipment.

"Oh, Mom, I'm glad you're not."

She threw me a dirty look.

"I mean, you should enjoy the party. Look how much you've had to do to get me to this point."

She smiled slowly, deeply. "Well, thanks, Violet." She added a wry edge. "I've certainly had my hands full."

"Just think, when the party's over and school's out, you'll be able to concentrate on starting your catering business."

She looked surprised to hear someone else say it, but

she nodded, punching a number into her calculator. "And I'll be hiring. Do you know of any teenage girls who might need a job?"

I flashed on Janell, Leda, and me, chopping up veggies and pulling stunts, laughing our heads off. And making money doing it.

"I might," I said, smiling.

Mom tossed her calculator in the grocery cart and hugged me, right in the middle of the frozen foods aisle.

★   ★   ★

A few days later, I tried my hand at making *frijoles negros* while Mom worked on her project at the kitchen table.

Mark sat next to her, flipping through a baseball magazine. "They don't smell like Abuela's beans," he complained.

"That's because they're not done yet," I said. They'd been cooking for hours, and they still looked kind of—crunchy.

Dad came in from work with his white coat over his arm, humming "Cielito Lindo."

"How was your day, *mi amor?*" Mom asked him.

Dad stopped his humming. "*¡Fantástico!* Great day!" He took a cigar from the refrigerator, unwrapped it, and stuck it, unlit, in his mouth. Rolled it around a little.

He did look happy, and more at ease than I'd seen him in a long time.

He took the cigar out and waved it at us. "Don't you want to know why I am so happy?" he coaxed.

The three of us waited.

"Drumroll, please."

This time I obliged until just past the point of annoyance.

"Violet, please. My news is: I got a new job."

Whoosh, our heads turned. We stared at him.

"You quit the Depot?" I asked, incredulous.

"I just gave notice."

Mom was shocked. "Without telling me?"

"I wanted to be certain," Dad said, smiling a good rendition of one of Abuelo's mile-long grins. "Day shift. Great bennies." He came over to the stove and looked in the bean pot with a squint, then waved a hand under his nose.

"That's great, Dad." I squeezed his shoulder.

"Will we have to move?" Mark said hopefully.

Dad shook his head. "Lincolnville Center Pharmacy. It's ten minutes closer to the house." He beamed. "Let's all go out to Red Lobster to celebrate."

"I'll go get dressed," Mom said, also not hungry for black beans for some reason. "Mark Edward Paz, when's the last time you combed your hair, young man?"

"Aw, it's baseball season!" Mark stomped off into the house behind Mom.

Dad rolled his Corona y Corona around in his mouth and puffed out happy little smoke-free breaths.

The Loco Family. *My* loco family: If you can't beat 'em, join 'em. I turned off the stove and went upstairs to get dressed.

33

The seasons had finally changed. Tulips and buds on the trees erased all memories of windchill factors and icy snow. Some called it spring. But for me, it was *quince* season.

Janell, Leda, and I sprawled in our usual niches in Janell's bedroom, reading. Pale spring sunshine bled through the sheers of the French doors, spotted by the shadows of jonquils dancing out in the wind. I'd just emerged unscathed from complete disaster in Caroline B. Cooney's *Flash Fire*. Janell was reading Sara Ryan's *Empress of the World*, the novel I'd given her for her birthday the week before, and who knew what trip Leda was on. I sat quietly in the window seat, not wanting to break the silence.

"Oh, man, would you listen to this!" Leda nearly capsized the beanbag chair. "Women are *still* only earning seventy-two cents on the dollar, compared to men!"

Janell and I raised our eyebrows at each other. She'd done it again.

"What's that?" I said to Leda.

"That's up from fifty-nine cents in 1970, the first year anybody gave enough of a damn to check, according to *Ms.* magazine." She looked back and forth between us. "It sucks being oppressed."

"I know," said Janell, shutting her book. "But what are you going to do about it?"

"I'll write a whole speech on it for Oratory next year!" Leda was already polishing a Declamation routine, cut from Mary Wollstonecraft's *A Vindication of the Rights of Woman,* which she planned to perform at my *quince.* Turns out if it's not assigned by a teacher, Leda doesn't mind homework.

"Well, you'd better have your other diatribe ready by the weekend for dress rehearsal, girl," I warned. Flora had agreed to let us use the dance studio space. "I'm as bad as The Ax when it comes to practicing. We're not going home until it's perfect."

"It will be perfect," said Janell.

We had revamped the program, turning "All the World's a Stage" into a fitting spectacle. To break the ice, I would start off with my Loco Family routine. That first performance slot always did give me an edge. Leda had accepted the challenge of following my spectacular act with her women's rights speech; then came my show tunes recital, and finally Janell would perform the dance/verse combination she'd put together.

Then the *quince*-babe would take center stage again. Dad and I could now dance a passable facsimile of a waltz, though at times we played the *timbales* with our knees. After the ceremonial dance, my *responsabilidades* would be over for the night and I could have some fun.

"I wish you would've let me invite Brian for my date," said Leda, the only guy-crazy vegetarian feminist activist I knew.

"Brian, from the rally? I thought you said he was a jerk and you gave him a fake phone number. Anyway, we're not doing dates," I reminded her yet again.

"Get out. You invited Clarence."

I *had* invited Clarence. "And his family, *idiota*. He's not my date. I just want him to be there."

"You want him to see you in that dress," said Janell, getting up from the rug and pulling her own gown out of the closet. "Aren't they fabulous?" She pressed the exotic sage-colored garment to her chest and pirouetted for us.

But Leda wasn't through with me. "By the way, Paz, how are you planning to fill yours out on top?" This, from the individual in present company with the least volume of chest. "Do you want to wear my Halloween bra?"

"What Halloween bra?"

"The 36D I stuffed with Styrofoam chips. You know, the one I wore with my costume? I think it's still under my bed."

"No, thanks, Leed. You can wear it."

She grimaced.

Janell smirked. " 'She's a woman phenomenally . . .' "

I sighed modestly and lifted my eyes to the ceiling. "'Phenomenal woman, that's me.'"

"Aaugh!" groaned Janell.

Leda threw her magazine at me.

★   ★   ★

Later that night, I sat in my room, just sort of drinking it all in. It was really going to happen. The hall was waiting, the tuxes were ordered, the out-of-town guests had confirmed. Amazingly, Mom's sister and parents would be flying in from Philly, and they had sent two large, silver-wrapped boxes for me. Abuela had shipped ahead the Miami furnishings that were too big to carry: an oversized guest book with a purple velvet cover and handmade-paper pages; several flat satin cushions in lilac meant for the gift display; and eighty-plus *capias,* party favors made of violet-hued ribbon, stamped with little, gold, smiling and frowning Janus masks. A gold inscription read, "*Todo el mundo, el teatro*–Violet Paz, 15 Years," and the date.

Not so many months ago, I hadn't even heard of any of this stuff. Now it gave me a thrill. But as the day approached, the old worries came scurrying in and out. I beat them back with a mental stick: I wouldn't be wearing a disgusting pink dress, I'd be in gorgeous costume. My speech was honed to perfection, and I'd even practiced a few Oscar-style words in appreciation of my sponsors. Bonus-plus: my little brother, who seemed to have grown a foot this year and was looking more and more like Dad, would not embarrass me. I had seen to that.

"So, *hermanito* of mine . . ." I hooked an arm around Mark's neck in the anonymity of the crowded airport as we waited for Abuela and Abuelo's plane to land. Dad was spending part of his birthday driving around in circles outside, to avoid parking. "You realize my *quince* is coming up."

Mark pulled a stupid face. "No! Re-e-eally?"

I kicked him and squeezed his neck harder. "As your older sister, I would like to request that you act on your best behavior." I gave him a doe-eyed look and let go of him. "Please. This is really important to me."

The light of Satan filled his eyes. "No problem-*o*," he lied in Spanglish.

"And don't wear your Cubs hat," I said, noticing that he wasn't wearing it now. The season had opened six weeks ago.

"No problem-*o*."

"And don't do anything stupid, or I'll—"

"Or you'll what?"

"Or," I said with my own devilish grin, "I'll tell Cathy Hennessy you like her." Mark seemed to have lost his aversion to the female sex along with his baseball cap, and I had filed the information away for blackmail purposes.

"Okay," he mumbled, staring out the floor-to-ceiling windows, suddenly fascinated by the guy in coveralls waving the plane in with those orange sticks.

"What'd you say, Mark?"

"Okay," he said through his teeth. "Your wish is my command."

"That's what I thought you'd say, little brother."

★　★　★

Abuelo was sleeping in, and Dad left for work, leaving Mom, Abuela, Mark, and me at the breakfast table.

I passed Abuela the sugar for her *café*.

"*Gracias,* Violeta," she said. If she was tired herself, you'd hardly know it. Eight-fifteen in the morning, and my grandmother looked fresh as a painted daisy in a crisp yellow cotton robe, creased in the sleeves. She had twisted her silver hair into an impeccable bun, trimming off any stray wisps. Since I'd seen her in September, she had discovered lip gloss, and today sported a shade and texture I'd call Cherry Tar Pit Slicker.

Mom finished her PowerBar and pushed away from the table. "I've got an accounting exam at nine o'clock." She leaned over to kiss Mark and me. To Abuela, she said, "I'll see you this afternoon." And off she went.

"I've gotta get going too," said Mark, gulping the rest of his milk. "Got someone to meet." He jumped up.

Abuela raised a black-penciled eyebrow at me. Before Mark could dash, she said, "*Un minuto,* mee-ster!"

"Huh?"

"Your dee-shes." She nodded for him to clear them away. "You are old enough to know better."

He did as she said, grabbed his books from the Death Throne, and bolted out the side door.

Way to go, Abuela! "I'm so glad you're here," I told her.

She smiled glossily. "Are you excited?"

"Um, yeah!" I answered, surprised it was so true. "It was really fun putting together the show. It's going to be great. And the dress, and the tiara . . . thanks, Abuela.

Thanks for getting me into this. If it weren't for you, I would never have known about *quinces*."

Her smile went awry. "Well, your father would not have been much help, *por supuesto*. I suppose that is my fault, a lee-tle bit."

"I thought you told Dad it was *his* fault if he wasn't paying attention while he was growing up."

She sighed. "I say that. But is the *mujer* who makes the tradition, always. For the men, *no tenemos expectaciones*. For why do you think the *quinceañero* exists only for the girls?"

I didn't know.

"Because is the woman who carries the tradition forward."

She paused.

"The man, he has the *tradición* in his blood. But is the woman who put it there, who make sure—how you say?— *que se viva*."

"That it lives on?"

"*Sí. Pero,* Alberto, he wanted to be different. The old ways were not for him. *Pues* . . ." She *tch*ed, her tongue sharp. "With your father, I could never say no, yes?"

We sat in silence a few moments.

"Anyway," she said, brightening, "tell me, Violeta. What are you going to do with your new *libertades*?"

"What new *libertades*?"

"*Pues*, the ones that go along with your *responsabilidades*, silly. Life is not all work and no fun, yes?"

Yes. Whatever she meant, I had a feeling she was right.

"When will you make your first *viaje*? Maybe coming to see Abuelo and me?"

A dim hope winged its way skyward. "Well—I'd like to go on the junior trip to Mexico next year. With my Spanish class."

Sticky lips framed a smile as bright as wildfire. "For the *clase de español*? This is wonderful!" Abuela had always wanted to be able to speak Spanish with me.

"Well, I won't exactly learn the whole language in seven days," I acknowledged. "Besides, I doubt if Dad will let me go."

"*¿Qué es esto?* Alberto won't let you go?" She muttered something else in Spanish too quickly and ferociously for me to interpret.

She patted my arm, looked me in the eye, and said, "*No te preocupes.* Leave it to me."

★　　★　　★

Later on, that night, a knock came at my door, and Dad stuck a brown polyester pants leg inside. "Violet?"

"Yeah, Dad." I pushed back from my desk.

"What're you doing?" he asked.

My social studies book lay untouched in front of me. "I'm—not much. Just sitting here."

"Sitting is good," he said, standing there, his fuchsia polo shirt clashing brilliantly with the dull house-paint brown of his pants.

"So, what are you up to?" I prompted.

"Well, I've got some journal reading to catch up on, and Mark wants me to fix the chain on his bike. And I have some ironing to do," he said, sitting down on my bed.

"You can put that off for a month or so," I teased, knowing he'd never let the ironing go.

"No, no!" he protested. "I'm going to get right down there." He picked at a pill on his pants.

"So. What is it, Dad? I know Abuela sent you in here."

I'd pulled the plug, and I watched his false nonchalance drain away.

"*Caramba,*" he complained, "she is like a tidal wave. She just keeps coming, and coming, and coming, until– *itan!*–you are flattened."

"I know what you mean," I said firmly.

He gazed up at the ceiling and studied a dark crack I'd made once while trying to smoosh a spider with a broom handle.

"What did Abuela do to you this time?" I asked, pretending I didn't already know. "Is there anything I can do to help?"

He looked at the crack another moment, then switched his gaze to me. "Yes. Yes, there is," he said. "You can find that permission slip for the Spanish trip and let me sign it."

"You mean the one to Mexico?"

"Yes, yes, that's the one. Even though you probably only want to go because all your friends are going. Young girls are like that, I suppose."

"All my friends aren't going," I corrected him. "I want to go see what another country is like."

He gave me a look that said, You've seen one, you've seen them all.

"And it would be neat to go someplace where everybody speaks Spanish, huh, Dad?" Sort of like *Cuba,* I didn't say.

The sound of the television drifted upstairs.

"I suppose it would."

I hesitated, then asked, "Do you remember anything about when you were a baby? Before you came here?"

He scowled. "I was only a little over a year old when we left the island. I don't remember anything." He amended, "Well, only bits and pieces. I have . . . little bits of images."

"Like–what?"

"Mmmm, the ocean, the color of the sea. The smell of the air . . . the way palm leaves flap in the wind." He paused. "How *guayaba* tastes."

"That sounds like a lot."

He didn't reply.

"I wish I could see it sometime."

He looked up through fierce eyes. "So do I," he said. "So do I."

I opened the desk drawer and fished around for the permission slip. It was stuffed in a corner. When I pulled it out, it looked wrinkled beyond repair.

Dad got up from the bed and came over. "Maybe we can iron it," he said, smoothing the edges with his fingers. Then something in the drawer caught his eye.

"What's this?" he asked, sliding a blue card out. It read, "No. 147599 THANK YOU _____ FOR YOUR 5/2 TAX-DEDUCTIBLE $5.00 DONATION, CLERGY FOR CUBA/PEACE WITH CUBA FOUNDATION." My raffle ticket. And beneath it, the leaflets I'd picked up at the rally. Dark clouds filled Dad's eyes as he scanned them.

"Can you explain these to me, young lady? 'Peace with Cuba'–that doesn't sound like Tibet." He shook the papers in my face. "Is this where you were last weekend?"

I stared at him.

"Well? Answer me!"

I gulped, not knowing what to say.

Slowly, he moved his head back and forth, a metronome of betrayal. "You lied. You lied to your mother and me?" he said with growing intensity. "*This* is what you go behind my back to do—getting involved with these political *sinvergüenzas*? If even one dime finds its way into Castro's hands . . ." He waved the confiscated papers. "*¡Óyeme!* Did Luz put you up to this?"

As these last words sank in, something in my heart—I don't know, snapped. Angry tears filled my eyes.

"No, Dad," I replied curtly, "*I* did it. I did it on my own. I wanted to see what was really going on." I spread my hands. "How am I supposed to learn anything about Cuba if you won't even let me try?"

Dad's face was full of fire. "This is precisely what I am trying to save you from, little girl!"

"*Dad.* I'm fifteen. I'm not a little girl anymore."

"And this is how you prove it? By lying to your parents? By stabbing your father in the back?"

I swallowed. "All I wanted was some information. You'll barely even mention the island! At least you were born there," I said bitterly. "The rest of us have to find out for ourselves what being Cuban is about."

He cocked his head. "Believe me, it is a long and winding road. And not an enjoyable one."

"See? Every time I bring up Cuba, this is what I get."

"That's because you're still too young to understand!"

I glared at him.

He held up the crumpled permission slip, fixing me with razor-sharp eyes. "So you think you can go off on some expensive trip to another country, thousands of miles away? You are far from being a responsible adult, *niñita*." He balled the paper up in his hand and added it to the rest of the contraband, muttering something in Spanish. "You stay here in your room until I call you."

He shut the door hard on his way out.

A wave of helplessness crashed over me. The tide had turned so suddenly. And none of this was my fault, I told myself.

I cried some, until the guilty feeling in my stomach was gone and only the anger remained.

3⁴

The chain of command had broken down. I was no longer a general or a *princesa* or a *quince*-babe, or anything else—just me, Violet Paz. And it was time to face the firing squad.

The real generals sat me down at the kitchen table: Mom, Abuela, and Abuelo, looking grave, and Dad, looking beyond disgusted. I scowled back at them.

Mom asked me to explain why I'd lied about the rally.

I avoided Dad's eyes. "It was just one of those 'peace with Cuba' deals," I said, playing my one card. "Does it really matter which country it was? You're for peace, right?" I asked the group.

"It's what I'm against that you should be worrying about," snapped Dad.

"Now, Albert . . . ," Mom murmured, though not pleased herself.

I tried to keep it simple. "How can peace be wrong? Explain that to me."

Dad and his parents exchanged looks.

"These groups," Dad began, "they *say* peace . . ."

"But they mean *comunismo*," Abuelo put in sourly. "These *grupos, siempre* they are hiding the real motive. There are many of them in Miami."

"*Qué descarados,*" added Abuela disparagingly.

"But these groups are legal, aren't they?" Mom asked. "Just as the anti-Castro groups are?"

"All this stuff is legal," I said. I knew this from the Web sites. "Right to assembly, free speech . . . And they aren't just a bunch of Communists." There were Democrats and Independents involved, lobbyists and housewives, bikers and schoolkids and clergymen. I'd seen their pictures, seen some of them in person at the rally. "Anyway, who's to say Communists don't also believe in peace?"

"Peace is one thing, Violet," Dad said through clenched teeth. "Political contributions are another." He waved the evidence.

"Come on, Dad! It was a five-dollar raffle ticket."

But to Dad, it was everything. "You *know* how I feel about Castro's government"—he nodded at Abuela and Abuelo—"how your grandparents have suffered, and yet you pull a stunt like this."

"And just when you are making your *quince,*" Abuela said in a voice strained to splinters.

"That's right!" Dad pointed a finger at me. "Look what you are doing to your grandmother. Maybe you don't deserve to have this *quince.* In fact," he said, nodding, "I think we should cancel it. What do you think, Diane?" he asked Mom.

Mom's green eyes were a sea of trouble. "Well, after this incident, I don't know. . . . Maybe she *isn't* mature enough. We could always send back the pledges. Return the gifts. Violet was the one who didn't want the party in the first place."

"*¿Qué?*" Abuela winced.

"Oh, that's just fine!" I muttered. "I finally figure out this *quince* deal and try to explore my Cuban roots and all that, and you suddenly tell me I'm too young to understand. So, what? I've been slaving away over the last nine months for nothing?"

Just then, Mark stuck his head in the kitchen. He must have been eavesdropping, and he saw me in the hot seat. "What happened to Violet?" he asked.

Mom blinked at him. "Upstairs, young man."

Mark froze.

"This doesn't concern you," snapped Dad.

Mark still didn't budge.

I blew out a hot breath. "Don't you get it? It does concern him. That's exactly what forced me to go around behind your backs, looking for answers."

"Answers to what?" asked my brother, even more curious now.

I glanced from Mark to Dad. "See?"

"That's it!" Dad threw up his hands. "We're calling the whole thing off."

A knife edged my gut, and I was surprised to feel it cut more with fear than with anger. I didn't want to lose this. I might not have seen the *quince* for what it was at first, but now I really, really wanted to go through with it. Needed it, somehow.

"You wouldn't take this away from me!"

"Don't think I won't!"

We locked eyes.

"Well, then," I said, "you'd be taking it away from yourselves too." I knew that Dad knew how much Abuela wanted this for me.

We all looked at Dad: Mark, jumping with questions; Mom, ready to yield. Abuelo edged closer to Dad. Abuela, her face a confusion of emotions, teetered somewhere in between.

Anything else I said would only get me in deeper.

Mom watched me wrestle in silence. "Let's think about it, Albert," she said.

★　★　★

Dad thought about it, all right, and he determined that Leda was my partner in crime. First, Mom spoke to Beth Lundquist, since Dad couldn't be trusted to be polite. She learned that I'd said yes, my parents knew where I was going that day—which was true, I pointed out. The community center in Aurora. This defense got me a pair of pursed lips and another stint in my room. I couldn't commiserate with Leda or Janell, whom I'd informed in the cafeteria earlier that day, because my phone and e-mail privileges were a thing of the past.

Then Dad blamed the public school system. It was Señora Wong, after all, who had got me started on my research. He even checked the family computer to see which Web sites I'd been frequenting. He stormed up and down and threatened to send me to boarding school. But even Mom, the scholar, didn't go along with that.

After dinner that evening, as everyone held their breath wondering who would be attacked next, the perfect scapegoat for Dad's ire walked in the front door: Tía Luci had arrived.

My heart sank when I saw how cheerful Luz was, excited about the music she'd brought for the *quince*–and unaware of the previous night's argument. She kissed Abuela and Abuelo and sat down next to them on the living room couch.

Usually, Dad was happy to see her. That day, she was the instigator of all evil.

"Well, if it isn't my well-meaning little save-the-world sister," he started in. "You're the one who got my daughter mixed up in these doings in the first place."

"Is there a problem?" Luz asked flatly.

Mom summed it up.

Luz turned her dark eyes on me. "Is that true?"

I nodded, feeling small at my perch on the piano bench. What would Luz have done if she'd been me? She would have just come out and said where she was going and let the dominoes fall where they might.

"I substituted Tibet for Cuba when I told Mom and

Dad," I said, "and I know that's wrong. And I'm sorry. But Dad never would have let me go, and there wasn't anything dangerous, or bad, or illegal, about it."

"That's also probably true," Luz assessed. "So what's at stake here?"

"I am thinking of calling off the party," said General Dad.

Again, Abuela looked pained, and I felt a sharp twinge inside. All her hard work.

"That seems excessive," Luz said. "She did say she was sorry."

Dad's wall of sternness didn't crack. "She also said she knew better. No thanks to you."

Luz ignored the slur. "It seems to me the real problem is Violet's interest in Cuba relations, not that she lied."

Abuela stepped in. "Interest is no the problem." She leaned forward. "Is the type of information she is getting."

Dad and Abuelo nodded.

"Well," Luz said, "with all those *cubanos* in one place, a *quince* party is the perfect place for a young woman to learn everything about Cuba, firsthand."

Touché.

Abuelo spoke up slowly. "*Pues,* punishment *o* no punishment, *tenemos otro problema,*" he said to Dad, patting Abuela's leg. "According to your *mamá* here, ees too late to cancel the rental of the hall."

This got Dad's attention. The ensuing discussion, full of its own roller coaster of ups and downs, determined that the party would have to go on. There were too many contributors and too much invested already.

"Well, Violet," said Dad with an angry sigh when it was all over, "you will have your little party. But this doesn't mean I condone your behavior. And I'll tell you one thing, *muchachita,*" he said, rising from his easy chair. "I won't be there."

★　★　★

I had to drag myself to dress rehearsal. What was the point? Without Dad, the whole show was fluff. Where there had been a meaning to things before, now there was just an empty hole. When I tried to beg off, Mom insisted I go through with the rehearsal and the party.

Seeing my friends throw themselves into their routines only made me feel worse. Mom sat in a corner of the studio, watching soberly as I danced the waltz with Señora Flora leading.

After we dropped Janell and Leda off, as we drove toward Woodtree Lane, Mom said quietly, "The party won't be the same without your father." She paused. "I hope you've learned something from this experience, Violet."

I was still feeling offended. "About how stubborn Dad is?"

Her face softened. "Stubborn, yes. But he feels bad about what's happened too."

"Then why make a big deal out of it?"

She considered this. "Your father is a very . . . principled man. Maybe a little too much so, sometimes." She turned a corner. "And maybe not entirely rightly so," she added. "But that is his business for him to handle."

"What if he's not handling it?"

"That's up to him."

We were silent a moment.

"So what's my business?"

"Your business," she said as we pulled into the driveway, "is being Violet, my dear." She shot me a look. "Whatever that entails."

35

The week went by with me not talking to Dad and Dad becoming very interested in the newspaper or the ceiling or his watch. We had never feuded like this. The Friday night before my *quince,* at dinner, Mom watched us studiously ignore each other. By the end of the meal, a new determination shone from her face.

The next afternoon, I sat with Mark, watching the Cubs game on WGN, trying to take my mind off the last few nights—and the next few days.

"You should've picked baseball as the theme for your keent-sy," Mark commented.

Not a bad idea.

"Then Abuela could've sewed you a Cubs uniform."

"She didn't sew anything, dummy."

"Whatever." Mark turned back to the TV.

It was one of those perfect spring days at Wrigley Field. Pennants waved on the scoreboard. The ivy was starting to creep in over the outfield wall. Four guys in the left-field bleachers had taken off their shirts, each chest smeared with a big blue letter: C-U-B-S. You just knew it was May. This was my kind of tradition.

I sighed. The world would be a better place if we could live by the rules of baseball. Where things are orderly and you know that strike two comes after strike one.

Dad walked in during the top half of the fourth, as the Cardinals were batting, and sat down in his chair, an unlit cigar in his hand. "Who's winning?" he asked.

I let Mark answer, "Cards, three-zip," and went on watching.

Dad cleared his throat. "*Oye,* Violet."

I edged my eyes his way.

"Your mother spoke to me again about coming to your party." He rotated the band around his cigar several times. "I want you to remember that this all came about because you lied to your mother and me. And while it is against my better judgment," he stated, "I said yes, I'll go."

He'd show, then.

I blew out a little breath. "It wouldn't be the same without you, Dad," I admitted.

He grew more serious. "But your mother and I expect you to be strictly honest with us in the future. And I want to have a talk with you about these peace organizations.

I'm not saying I'll like what they have to say . . . ," he warned.

It couldn't be that easy. "But—will you dance with me? At the party?"

He looked at me a moment. *"Sí."*

A smile snuck past my lips.

"But only because your grandmother and grandfather have put so much into this. And many of your relatives. And because your mother asked me to." He stuck the cigar in his mouth.

"Are those the only reasons?"

He removed the cigar. "Well . . . it's true, Violeta, that you are growing up. I guess I have to face facts. And while you and I may not always agree on everything, you are entitled to your own opinion."

I knew those were Mom's words, but as my eyes widened, he added, "Besides . . . I wouldn't want to miss my daughter's one and only *quinceañero,* would I?" He smiled.

I did too.

"And another thing . . ."

"What?"

"Well . . ." He took a deep breath. "Maybe we should talk a little bit about Cuba sometime. You and me and Mark."

I goggled at him. "We—should?"

"If there's something special you want to know."

"That's be great, Dad." I went over and hugged him.

Mark quit pretending he wasn't listening. "Do I still have to go to the keent-sy?" he asked.

"Yes!" Dad and I both said.

We went on watching the game together, but inside I marveled. The tide had turned again, this time with Mom's help, I was sure. She had stuck up for me with Dad, had pushed him a little farther than ever before. School was good for Mom. She was ... braver now. Maybe it would rub off on me.

★　★　★

That night, the phone rang. It was Janell.

"Hang on a second while I get Leda." She put me on hold. "Okay. There."

"Hello? Am I on?" came Leda's voice.

"I'm using the three-way calling," Janell said.

"Cool," I replied, suddenly nervous, realizing that the next time I saw them would be onstage.

"We just wanted to wish you luck," my friend since the first grade said.

"That's right, Paz," seconded Leda. "It's time for your passage from 'the girl onto the woman.' "

I grinned, remembering where she'd gotten the phrase. I was done with *Quinceañero for the Gringo Dummy;* I'd graduated and given the book to Leda, who'd finally gotten her period. Beth and Niles had agreed to celebrate Leda's *quince* in August, with a Norse twist. And I thought my ceremony was nontraditional.

"So how are you doing?" she asked. "Got the jitters?"

My stomach caved in all over again. "Thanks a lot! Hey, guess what? Dad's decided to dance with me after all."

"That's great news," said Janell. "Look, Violet, whether

your dad's there or not, we just wanted to let you know, don't worry about tomorrow. We'll be there for you."

"Yeah," Leda added. "We've got your back."

My stomach was flattered. "Gee, thanks, guys. I–don't know what to say. I guess I'll just go out there tomorrow and die trying."

"You will not die trying! You will . . . *triumph* trying," corrected Janell. "You can do it, woman."

"That's right," said Leda. "You remember your speech, don't you?"

I started to wail again, but she cut in. "Of course you do. You've practiced it like crazy. Now, you go out there tomorrow, and kick some big, hairy *quince* ass!"

"We'll see you tomorrow, girlfriend," said Janell.

"Hasta mañana," I said, and hung on to the phone a minute, waiting until I heard both clicks before putting it down.

36

*O*n Sunday morning, tendrils of bacon smoke and the smell of frying bananas climbed the stairs to my room and tapped on the door. *"You better come on in my kitchen . . . 'cause it's going to be raining outdoors . . . ,"* Robert Johnson sang to me from the downstairs tape player. I stretched and got out of bed quick. Took another sniff. Alert the media: Dad was cooking.

Even Abuelo was up before me; the main cast of the Loco Family greeted me from the kitchen table, saving the Death Throne for me. I slipped into Dad's chair while he finished making breakfast.

"Cuban pancakes, my favorite. Thanks," I said,

accepting a glass of juice from Mom. Chucho followed her around the kitchen, then returned to his post next to the chef.

Dad's signature dish made rare appearances in the Paz kitchen, always greeted with near-rabid anticipation. Fried-banana-and-bacon pancakes, topped with whipped butter, toasted coconut flakes, and a healthy ladle of "Señora Butterworth's." *¡Ay, ay, ay!*

Or, as Abuelo said after his first bite, giving a little drumroll, *"¡Riquísimo!"*

The salty bacon plays perfectly off the fried-in-butter banana bits, prompting us all to wonder at one time or another why we've never seen the dish on the menu in fancy restaurants. That may be because we don't visit fancy restaurants much. Or it may be because the American Heart Association would outlaw the combination. In any case, Dad claims it's the only thing he can cook.

"And how is the *quinceañera* today?" asked my grand-mother, already dressed in a skirt and blouse and made up as if the Shriners' Circus were in town.

"Estoy muy bien, gracias," I said, sticking a finger in the pool of syrup on Mark's plate and tasting it.

"Hey–!" he began, then noticed my look. "Dear sister," he added. "All ready for your keent-sy?"

I nodded, mainly ready for pancakes.

Mom, next in line, took her plate from beside the stove and sat down. "Someone has to call the florist's hotline to check on the Sunday delivery, or they might forget. Mark, please take Chucho for his run when you're finished. And be dressed for church by eleven!"

Father Leone was going to have a coronary: The entire Paz clan would be at Mass at St. Edna's today, including my aunt Luz, who was staying with an old grade-school friend nearby.

Dad, decked out in his seldom-used I HATE TO COOK apron, brought my short stack to the table and set the plate before me. I started to switch seats, but he said, "No, no. You eat there, and enjoy. I'll stand." Even Dad knew better than to tackle the Death Throne. He retreated to the stove to flip some more pancakes.

I poured on some syrup and took a bite. "God, Dad, these are great!"

"I made them special for the *quinceañera*," he said, smiling proudly, though whether over my *quince* or his cooking, I couldn't tell.

When we'd all had our fill, we lingered around the table burping bacony breaths and finishing coffee or juice. Chucho got bored searching for cast-off food particles and started pestering Mark for his walk, so they took off.

"*Ah-cha!*" Abuelo swallowed the murky *café* dregs in his demitasse and pushed his chair back. "Is another hour before we go to *la iglesia*," he said innocently. "I wonder what is there to do."

One by one, we clapped eyes on him.

"*¡Corramos!*"

He leapt up, getting a head start, and we all raced after him—Dad slowing to grab two Coronas from the fridge—down the hallway and through the sliding door to the players' porch. God, Father Leone, and my *quinceañero* would have to wait. The Paz family had a domino match to play.

We took two cars to church and split up afterward. The men went home to heat up some leftover *congrís;* the women drove to the banquet hall to meet Señora Flora.

Leda and Janell were already there, carrying out Flora's instructions for seating arrangements and table decorations. It felt good seeing my *damas de honor* perform some honest work on my behalf.

"Wow! It looks fantastic in here. Thanks, you guys," I said, really meaning it. "I'd do the same for you."

"Yes, you will," warned Leda.

"Right, right. In August." I grinned.

Flora trotted up to Mom, Abuela, and me looking uncharacteristically strained. "Ladies, I'm so glad you're here. We have caterers, we have cake, we have a sound system, but no flowers. *¿Donde están las flores?*"

Abuela raised her eyebrows at me. I looked accusingly at Mom.

Mom slapped her forehead with a palm. "I knew there was something else . . ." She fished through her purse for the florist's phone number, in vain, then practically prostrated herself at Flora's feet. "I should have let you handle the flowers, but Salma promised us such a discount. . . ."

Abuela came through with the listing in her electronic notebook, and Flora handed Mom her cellular phone.

"No answer!" She grabbed my hand. "Come on, Violet, we'll dash over to the shop. You girls, stay here and hold the fort," she said to everyone else.

Mom drove across town like one of Sammy Sosa's homers on its way out of the park. We screeched to a stop in front of Flores R Us and banged on the door, but the shop was closed up tight as a rosebud.

There was nothing to do but get back in the car. Mom sat there with her hands gripping the steering wheel, keys dangling from the ignition, berating herself. "I should've known I could never juggle school and kids and parties and everything else too. I'm just a disaster, a disaster, I tell you." And on and on.

"Mom, Mom," I cut in. "Chill. You're doing fine. If it weren't for you, we wouldn't even be having a party." I patted her shoulder. "Let's just get back to the hall. I'm sure Señora Flora can . . . nip this in the *bud*."

She looked at me, unconvinced.

I tried again. "We have better things to do than play ring around the *posy*."

She held desperately to her frown, which was melting like cheap sealing wax.

And the two-oh pitch: "I say, let's put the *petal* to the metal and get out of here!"

A smile laminated her face. *"HA!"* she barked, followed by three involuntary tremors. "Petal to the metal. That's a good one, Vi."

She fastened her seat belt, put the car in gear, and took us back across Lincolnville under the speed limit.

★　★　★

When we returned to the hall, the flowers had arrived— hundreds of purple and white irises. My backstage contingent was madly stuffing them into glass vases.

"Look, Violet! The stage is set up," Janell said, breaking away and dragging me to the large riser hung with a purple theater curtain. Flora had really outdone herself. A rented crystal chandelier hung above a white baby grand piano upstage. Colored spotlights shone from the ceiling, and a huge relief map of the world acted as backdrop.

"It's beautiful," I said, squeezing Janell's hand. "I can't wait to get in costume."

I didn't have to wait.

"Violet!" called Mom. "Time to go home and change."

So she and Abuela and I drove back home.

We arrived to find the men serenely watching the Cubs play the Cards again on TV. "Why aren't any of you dressed!" Mom yelled.

"Is plenty of time," said Abuelo, who would be wearing a new white *guayabera* and trousers. I had reminded him to wear shoes, not slippers.

"Sammy's on deck," argued Mark, who would be wearing a white-on-white tuxedo with black accents, a white boutonniere, and no Cubs hat.

"*Maldito* monkey suit," Dad muttered, leaning forward to watch someone get thrown out at second. He would be dressed just like Mark.

Mom didn't have to say a word. Her glare erupted, venting hot steam and shooting fiery molten lava at the three of them—a look promising a quick ticket to hell. They reacted appropriately.

"On second thought," said Abuelo, rising, "I should be going."

"It might take a couple tries to get my bow tie right," murmured Dad.

Mark just ran.

37

When I came downstairs in my dress, Mom, Mark, Abuela, and Abuelo were waiting.

"*Ay, qué bonita,*" said Abuelo, kissing my cheeks.

"*¡Magnífica!*" Abuela exclaimed.

Mom took my hands and held me at arm's length. "It's you, dear," she said softly.

"Where's Dad?"

"Why don't you run back upstairs and see what's keeping him?"

I flew on my purple-dyed ballet slippers and planted a knock on Dad's bedroom door. "Dad?"

No answer.

"Dad?"

He opened the door in his white tuxedo pants and a T-shirt, a mournful expression on his face. "I can't go on," he whispered.

"What are you talking about?"

"I can't go onstage and dance with you."

"If it's about last week . . ."

"No." He pushed the door open and gestured me in, looking like he was about to cry. "I came out of the shower to . . . to–this." He pointed at the bed, where his tuxedo shirt and jacket were laid out.

There, alongside the rented clothing, stretched Chucho's colorless, hairy mass. The industrious poodle took no notice of either of us as he methodically finished picking off and swallowing down the last of the row of shiny black tuxedo buttons.

Dad stood, beaten, frozen to the carpet. I had to think fast.

"No te preocupes," I told him. "Here's what we'll do . . ."

★   ★   ★

When we were all packed into Mom's minivan, I remembered something at the last second.

"My tiara!"

I ran back inside to get the velvet bag. On the way out, I caught sight of myself in the hall mirror. It was like one of those moments when you see your reflection in a store window, and not realizing it's you, say to yourself, She's looking *good*! And then you go, Hey, that's me!

I'd scrutinized myself earlier, getting my hair and makeup right, tugging my gown on straight. Making sure I wore matching socks—just kidding. But all of a sudden, here was this stranger's view of me. And you know what? I looked pretty darn good.

It wasn't just looks, though. If I wasn't mistaken, for a moment there you might say I had a certain . . . presence. I smiled at myself in the mirror.

"Who's on first," I murmured.

Dad honked impatiently outside.

★ ★ ★

At last, I sat alone backstage, out of sight, waiting for the guests to arrive and sign in. Leda and Janell were busy greeting people at the door while my family held court at our table. Señora Flora was off helping the caterers prepare.

"Violet? Are you in there?" My aunt Luz slipped behind the curtain. "Vi, you look beautiful!" Luz looked pretty sexy herself in a long black evening gown scattered with delicate red flowers. She wore a few gold bangles on her bare arms, and her black hair hung to her waist in refined curls.

I got up and hugged her. "Thanks for being here, Tía Luci. I am *so* nervous."

"A little bit nervous is good," Tía counseled. "I just want to say happy fifteen, *chica*. I hope it's everything you dreamed of."

"Nope. It's better. You never get to eat as much cake as you want in your dreams."

"Maybe not in *your* dreams," she teased. "Well, I hope you like the music. I'm going to make a live recording."

"Awesome," I said, feeling the spark of readiness.

She air-kissed my cheek. "Break a leg, kiddo," she said, and slipped back out.

I went over and did something I'd always wanted to do, peeked through the curtain at the gathering house. It looked like the setting for a big production. My relatives on both sides–the Chicago-area Cubans and the Philly contingent–were dressed to the nines. It was great to see Grandma and Grandpa Shavlovsky laughing with Abuela and Abuelo, and odd to see my piano teacher, Mrs. Lowenstein, swathed in a shiny blue cocktail dress. She gravitated over to Luz's sound board, and they fell deep in conversation.

I was surprised to see Mark quietly chatting with a cousin, until I recognized her as Celina, Eva's little sister with the fashion-model face and the beginnings of a figure that hinted at greatness. Mark looked different in his tux. Maybe even *elegante*. My worm of a brother seemed to have a modicum of taste; maybe he wouldn't grow up to be too much like Dad.

The Lundquists and Williamses and Janell's mom all sat together, talking as though they'd known each other forever. And Clarence looked Fine, with a capital *F*, in a tan suit and new buzz cut. Seeing the other faces I didn't know as well was a little scary–I had to make these people laugh, after all. But then I remembered that most of them had invested money in this affair, so they must have held a reasonable expectation of getting some return on their dollar. If they didn't like my routine, they could always ask Dad for their money back. They were used to him making change.

Dad. I half expected to see him winding through the crowd with his coin pouch, handing out dimes and cigars. I picked him out of the knot of people standing around our table. I had never seen him looking so stylish as in the well-cut tuxedo suit. He had unnecessarily shined the white patent leather shoes the night before, and ironed his white socks and T-shirt twice. He was the picture of fashion co-ordination, from the white bow tie, which Mom had tied, to the white buttonless coat and creased pants. Except for one minor detail.

In place of the de rigueur pleated white tuxedo shirt, which Chucho had divested of its buttons, Dad wore his fa-vorite sunshine-yellow long-sleeved good-luck shirt with the multicolored monkeys printed on it. Improvisation, I called it.

I skimmed over my lines. "The story you are about to hear is true. . . . The story you are about to hear is true. . . ."

Now Leda and Janell came jostling through the curtain.

"Three minutes," whispered Janell.

"Remind me again why we have to do this?" Leda said, suddenly all nerves.

I rolled my eyes at her and shrugged helplessly.

"Here," said Janell, "let me help you put your crown on." She pulled the jeweled tiara from its velvet bag and set it on my head, adjusting it a few times.

"Perfect," Leda pronounced.

I reached into my purse for a sugar cube, and some-thing rustled. I drew out a narrow sheet of paper alive with crinkles that somebody had done their best to smooth out. My permission slip for the trip—and it was signed.

Dad! He'd signed his full name in formal-looking script in blue ink:

Alberto Ricardo Paz

I drew a sharp breath, turning the flattened page over in my hand. I couldn't be sure, but it looked like he'd ironed it!

I smiled.

As Luz set the tone with a recorded fanfare of trumpets, the house lights dimmed.

"Let's go, Violet," whispered Leda, dragging me stage right to the wings. "This is it!"

Out front, Señora Flora quieted the guests. "*Bienvenidos,* everybody, and welcome to the *quinceañero* for a girl who is very near and dear to your hearts. Please give a big hand to a young woman who has learned in her fifteen years what took Guillermo Shakespeare nearly a lifetime to know: that all the world's a stage."

I popped the sugar cube in my mouth.

"Ladies and gentlemen, please welcome your very own . . . Violet Paz!"

The curtain parted magically.

I hesitated, one beat, two. I hesitated just long enough to make my *damas* worry, so that together they gave me a strong push from the wings.

I let out a siren wail and zigzagged across the stage like I was being chased by the Spanish Inquisition. My tiara started to slip, but I righted it. Then I hit my mark and froze, making eye contact with the roomful of friends and family. A single spotlight illuminated me.

The audience looked back, speechless, riveted—faces I

knew, faces I didn't know . . . here, for me. Funny how so much in life can swirl around you, I thought, whole traditions and civilizations you know nothing about until someone points them out.

The sugar cube let me zip ahead of my thoughts, collect myself, even recall the lines I'd rehearsed so many times.

I took a deep breath, opened my mouth, and let the truth come out.

About the Author

NANCY OSA reads, writes, thinks, blasts blues music, and communes with nature in and around Portland, Oregon. Visit her at www.nancyosa.com.